THE MYSTERIOUS WU FANG:
THE CASE OF THE SIX COFFINS

THE CASE OF
THE SIX COFFINS

By Robert J. Hogan

ALTUS PRESS • 2016

CHAPTER 1
EMPEROR OF DEATH

THE KEEN ears of Wu Fang, Dragon Lord of Crime and Emperor of Death, had detected something—a sound of softly padding footsteps that came down the dark winding passage leading to his underground room at the bottom of London's Limehouse.

As his ears caught that significant sound, he smiled faintly and spoke to himself. His voice was surprisingly mild and kindly, considering the cruel yellow lips that uttered the syllables.

"Ah," he said, "Wu Fang does not wait in vain. Is Hurdan back from America? He will have, of course, what he promised to bring."

The soft padding of footsteps grew louder, loud enough for the ears of an ordinary man to catch, had he been unfortunate enough to be there.

A slight draft wafted through the open doorway from the corridor and the musty, foul smell that it brought with it mingled strangely with the faint, Oriental incensed air of the dim room.

Suddenly, the expression of anticipation faded from the face of Wu Fang and a frown puckered the skin of his ample forehead.

"But they are not the footsteps of Hurdan," Wu Fang breathed. "They belong to someone else, an enemy perhaps."

He stepped quickly to the side of the room and stood before

"Now," said Wu Fang, "I believe we are about ready for my little murder agents."

an elaborately embroidered tapestry that adorned the otherwise blank wall.

"Baru, my little poison one, you will be ready if I give the command."

As though in answer, the tapestry moved ever so slightly.

Wu Fang walked back to the center of the room and took his stand before a great, heavily-carved desk facing the door.

He was a tall yellow man with slim, drooping shoulders from which hung a mandarin robe of embroidered yellow silk. His long-fingernailed hands were clasped loosely behind him. His movements were profoundly dignified and deliberate like those of a kindly old doctor or college professor.

His slanting eyes had widened now as they watched the open doorway and there was a strange light in the jade-green pupils that made them almost iridescent, like the eyes of a cat in the darkness.

Around the first turn of the inky corridor, the footsteps came. Then a figure emerged from the darkness, a ghastly figure of a man stark naked except for a loin cloth. He was dark-skinned with spindly legs, a pot-belly, wide shoulders, powerful arms, and a flat head.

The eyes of Wu Fang gleamed still more brightly as he looked at that figure.

"Yacun," he said, but there was no anger or surprise in his voice. "What are you doing here? Where is Hurdan?"

The naked man fell down before the tall figure and went through the ceremony of kissing the Oriental shoes that Wu Fang wore.

The Dragon Lord waited patiently.

"Rise and answer, Yacun," he commanded.

The dark-skinned man obeyed.

"Master, I am sorry. I have bad news," he said in a rasping voice that was scarcely audible.

Wu Fang nodded very slowly.

"Wu Fang waits for more words, Yacun."

The naked man brought forward a bottle around which was wrapped a piece of paper.

"This is all, master," he said.

Wu Fang's eyes narrowed.

"All?" he asked. "But you have not yet answered my question about Hurdan."

"I will tell you, master," Yacun hurried on. As he talked, sweat

4

oozed from his pores. It was apparent that he was not accustomed to facing the Emperor of Death.

"It was nearly a complete success, master. Hurdan and I were at the dock in New York, getting on the boat. I was going up the gangplank first Hurdan was following me. He was carrying the bottle on his person for safety. Then the one who had been trailing us reached us. He grappled with Hurdan, found the bottle. Hurdan did his best, master. When he saw he could not get away he threw the bottle into the water. It was at night. I dived instantly and recovered it. I knew the people on the ship would be searching for us now, but the darkness permitted me to stow myself away on the boat. When the ship docked, I slipped overboard and swam here to the secret passage that Hurdan had told me about."

Again Wu Fang nodded slowly, thoughtfully. He was holding the glass bottle in his hand, staring down at it.

"And Hurdan, he was killed?"

"Yes, master."

"That is a pity. But he did his work well."

"But master," Yacum objected. "The mission was not a success."

The Chinaman shrugged his shoulders.

"Have I not the liquid that I sought, and the note?"

"You have the liquid, master," Yacun agreed, "but of the note you have only half. The other part must have been torn away in the struggle with the police officer."

The long-nailed fingers of Wu Fang worked suddenly as he slipped off two rubber bands that held the piece of crumpled paper to the glass bottle. With lightning speed, he opened the crumpled paper.

Yacun had spoken the truth. Wu Fang held in his hands a bottle of clear, syrupy liquid and a note that had been torn through the middle. The note was written in code, but he translated what remained of it at a glance:

> From what I can learn, this
> a colorless gas when expo
> some mysterious action on
> him dead in a few hours.
> wide area and lie there
> wind is not too strong
> inventor is George Op

"Yes, I see, Yacun," he nodded gravely after reading the contents. "That does not make it any too clear."

He lifted his eyes from the note now and the green light flashed once more on Yacun's dark face.

"This one who killed Hurdan," he asked. "You know who he is?"

"Yes," nodded the other. "It was a government man who had been sent to follow us. It was Val Kildare."

The voice of Wu Fang came softly and more kindly than usual, but there was an added flash of green in his eyes that revealed his bitter hatred.

"The curse of a thousand demons will be his fate. You have done your work well, Yacun. You shall be justly rewarded. That is all."

YACUN LEFT the way he had come. Wu Fang saw him close the door behind him, then he lifted the telephone and pressed one of the many buttons on the desk top.

"There is one Val Kildare, United States government agent," he said when a voice answered. "It is my wish that he die the most painful death that is in our power to inflict. Do you understand?"

He pressed another button, and when a second agent spoke, gave further orders.

"You will come at once. It is important."

Without waiting for a response, he hung up the phone. Then he sat down in the great chair before the desk and assumed a rather pious posture. He brought his hands together and separated them slowly, deliberately. Finger-tips touched fingertips. He was careful not to damage the long fingernails that extended from them; his green eyes were upon those fingers. He remained in that position until a knock sounded at the door.

"Come in," he commanded without turning.

The door opened and a neatly attired white man entered. He was suave in his greeting. His features, bearing and expression were strikingly British.

"Eaton," Wu Fang said, "I have a special mission for you tonight. There is a little village of Chessfield north of here. You know the place?"

A startled look came into the eyes of the Englishman.

"Quite, sir," he nodded.

"Very well," Fu Wang went on. "You are to charter a plane.

He watched the Englishman as his
words broke off in a scream of pain.

You see this bottle of liquid on the table? I wish you to drop it
in the center of Chessfield as the pilot flies over it. Do you
understand?"

Eaton's face went white.

"Good Lord, sir," he gasped. "Is it something that will kill?"

"That is my affair," Wu Fang replied coldly.

"But you see, I can't do it," Eaton hurried on. "My mother and sister both live there. Why, confound it, I was born there."

"Then, perhaps," Wu Fang ventured, "I should name another town nearby. Let us say Endham."

"But, I say," the Englishman protested. "Can't you choose another place? I have friends in Endham."

The green eyes shot sparks for a moment, but other than that, Wu Fang showed no change in his kindly demeanor.

"Let me think," he said. "Do you know where a town called—"

Suddenly he whirled toward the tapestry and raised his voice so that it filled the room. "Baru, you will strike now."

Eaton, who stood with his back toward the tapestry, looked perplexed for a moment. He opened his mouth to speak.

From below the tapestry something shadowy slithered without making a sound. At first glance it might have looked like a mouse running at top speed over the Chinese rug but it was a bit larger and, although it seemed to run on legs, it wriggled at the same time like a snake.

"I say, sir," Eaton began, "I don't recall ever having heard of—"

But just as he reached that point, the strange little beast that Wu Fang had called Baru, reached Eaton's left foot and disappeared inside his trouser leg. The Englishman's words broke off in a gasped scream of terror and pain. Then his cry died to an insane gurgle, he stiffened like a ramrod and fell over backward.

Wu Fang smiled as his green eyes followed the tiny beast which was even now running back to its hiding place. Then his hand moved and he pressed another button.

A few minutes later, a dark young man entered. He also was neatly attired, but unlike Eaton, his features bespoke Latin blood.

Wu Fang watched silently as the newcomer eyed the body on the floor.

"*Man dieu,* monsieur," he gasped, "he looks—dead."

"Yes," Wu Fang nodded. "I trust so, Le Tour. But listen to me now so that you may escape the same fate. You know where the village of Chessfield is located?"

Le Tour got control of himself with apparent effort. He nodded.

"*Oui,* monsieur," he said.

"Do you see this bottle on the desk?" Wu Fang asked. "I wish you to charter a plane, now for tonight. Have the pilot fly over Chessfield and drop this bottle into the center of the village."

He shifted his glance significantly toward the still, stiff form of Eaton on the floor. "You have no objections, Le Tour?" he added.

"No, no, of course not, monsieur," Le Tour answered hastily.

"Very well," Wu Fang nodded. "I will consider that it is already done. That is all."

Wu Fang clapped his hands twice as Le Tour left the room. Almost instantly, two stalwart Chinamen entered and stood motionless before him. Their faces were like expressionless masks.

The tall man uttered no words. His green eyes flashed to Eaton's body and then to the door. A moment later the two

men were gone—with the body of the English agent who had
had scruples against killing his own flesh and blood.

The door closed softly behind them. Wu Fang reached for
the phone and spoke into it again.

"I wish to motor into the country exactly fifteen minutes
before dawn. Until then I will not be disturbed."

Hanging up the receiver, he leaned back in the great carved
chair and closed his eyes.

The yellow man with the brain of a super-human must have
exercised his own power upon himself for he fell instantly asleep.
He slept soundly without the slightest movement.

THE NIGHT wore on into early morning. It was less than
a half hour before dawn, when, as though an accurate alarm
clock had given him warning, he opened his eyes. And now
that his eyes were open there was no sign of lingering drowsi-
ness. He was awake as quickly as he had fallen asleep a few
hours before.

He rose from his chair, went into another room, and within
a few minutes had, with the aid of two servants, dressed himself
in Occidental garb. With tinted glasses covering his eyes he
looked not at all unlike the average business man on the streets
of London.

He strode softly through a winding, dank smelling corridor,
up two flights of stairs and out into the street through the back
end of a curio shop.

A long black town car drove up at the moment he made his
appearance. He stepped inside quickly, sank from sight behind
the long, windowless rear sides of the auto, and the car moved

on. The long-nailed hands, which had been thrust into the pockets of his business suit when he left the curio shop, came into view now; one of them reached for the speaking tube.

"You will drive me to the cliffs overlooking the village of Chessfield," Wu Fang ordered.

The liveried chauffeur nodded without turning. "Yes, master," he said quietly. It grew light as they rolled out of the squalor of Limehouse, through finer sections and then into the suburbs. As the sun disced up in the east they gradually climbed to higher ground. When they topped the cliffs overlooking Chessfield the sun was gleaming into the valley below.

Again Wu Fang spoke into the tube.

"You will stop here."

The car pulled to the left side of the road at a spot that permitted a good view of the valley.

Wu Fang adjusted a pair of powerful binoculars before his eyes, lowered the window so that his view would not be obstructed.

He smiled slightly.

Now he would see the results of his little experiment. It was unfortunate that part of the note containing information had been snatched by Val Kildare. But as it was in code the American could not read it and anyway it would not be with him for long. Wu Fang's agents would see to that.

He sat up a bit straighter.

A cottage door in the village below had opened and several people had come out.

They were reeling drunkenly. Wu Fang smiled.

"The liquid is working nicely," he breathed.

Then he spied two figures lying at the doorstep of another house. One—a woman—seemed to be crawling toward the other, who was a man. Perhaps her husband. To anyone else, the sight would have been a pitiful one. A wife trying to help her husband—and both dying out there in the street. Dying from some cause they could not understand.

But Wu Fang smiled more broadly.

Other people were coming into view now. As the sun rose higher over the town the houses and cottages were belching their occupants into the streets wholesale.

Human beings writhed on the pavements. Some stumbled out to land on their knees and there to pray—only to fall prostrate a few minutes later.

At the edge of the village Wu Fang saw a gray-haired woman stagger from the door of a cottage. She half ran, half reeled down the flower-lined path that led to the gate. And there she fell, clutching to the gate desperately and reaching one hand up to heaven in a manner of supplication.

A younger woman followed. But before she could reach the older woman she stumbled and fell forward, clutching at the flowers beside her and pulling them up by the roots.

"Probably the mother and sister of Eaton," Wu Fang breathed, shaking his head sadly. "It is a pity—but necessary. Wu Fang must learn the full name of the inventor from whom Hurdan stole that bottle. Undoubtedly it is contained in the other half of the note and most probably the inventor lives in New York."

The yellow fiend watched for several more minutes. Watched until no more people came staggering from their houses to die.

Then he counted the bodies lying in the streets.

"Almost two hundred of them. That is quick work indeed. And why would not this liquid snuff out millions of lives just as easily—if it could be spread in cities like London and New York!"

He raised the window, put away his glasses and gave order to the driver to return.

Less than an hour later he was seated at his heavily carved desk in the underground room, talking on the phone.

"You will prepare to go to New York at once," he said. "We leave on the next steamer. Take full precautions and all necessary persons and equipment. The experiment was a success. We must now obtain the other half of the message from Mr. Val Kildare who undoubtedly still has it. Tell the agents who attack Mr. Kildare to be very careful to find the note before they permit his body to be disposed of."

Wu Fang's general at the other end of the line answered.

"A thousand pardons, but I have bad news. We have not yet been able to reach Kildare, although he is here now in London."

The green eyes of Wu Fang shot fire for a moment, but his voice was calm.

"Very well," he said. "Do your best. Do you know where he is at the present moment?"

"Yes," replied the other. "He has just left his hotel with a special guard from Scotland Yard to investigate the mysterious death of all the inhabitants of Chessfield this morning."

Wu Fang smiled.

"I trust he will find the investigation interesting. When is the next steamer leaving for New York?"

There was a brief pause, then: "It is The Bergenland. It leaves tomorrow night at ten o'clock."

"Very well," Wu Fang finished. "We will sail for America on The Bergenland at ten tomorrow night."

CHAPTER 2
CARGO OF CORPSES

FOR ALMOST twenty-four hours after The Bergenland left her docks bound for New York, Jerry Hazard had kept pretty much to himself. It was late afternoon of the first day out when the foreign correspondent completed typing his news story. He pulled the last revised sheet of paper from his portable typewriter and got up.

The room seemed to swim about him as he took his eyes from the paper where they had been focused for so long. He grasped the edge of his bunk to steady himself. Then, just as he got his balance, the floor came up with a steady, gradual heave that seemed to have no end.

Jerry Hazard stood up to his full height of nearly six feet and squared his broad shoulders. A queer sensation stole over him. Tiny beads of perspiration were oozing out on his forehead; he felt hot and cold by spells. He spoke aloud to himself; there was no one else in the stateroom.

"Phew!" he said. "Old Man Ocean has sure got sore about something. Funny, I didn't notice it before."

Turning, he glanced at his firmly-chiseled face in the mirror over the lavatory at the deck end of the cabin.

"So you can't take it, eh, Jerry?" he grinned at himself, rather sheepishly. "Old Man Ocean has done got you down. I was all right as long as my work was holding my interest. Better get out on deck for awhile."

He slipped on his coat, gathered up the three sheets of paper that he had been laboring over for so long, and stepped out of his cabin. With the characteristic carelessness of newspapermen, he didn't bother to lock it.

Holding the large, silken cord that was strung along one side of the corridor, he steadied himself against the heavy roll of The Bergenland; and at the first opportunity, stepped out on deck. The open air felt better. He threw out his chest and inhaled deeply.

"Swell!" he breathed. "That's more like it."

The sky was ominously dark and the wind was blowing across the decks at a fast clip. It cut into him with a sting of icy fingers; sprays of hard-driven rain smacked his face. But he walked along briskly until he reached the wireless room.

Here he handed his story to the operator and paid for its transmission to the New York office of his syndicate.

"Rotten weather," he ventured, as he turned to go. "Think it will get worse?"

The wireless operator glanced out of his window, gave a short nod.

"I wouldn't be surprised," he announced. "We're in for a rough crossing if the sailor's signs mean anything."

Jerry Hazard

"What do you mean, sailor's signs?" Hazard queried. "You don't mean to tell me that people believe in sailor's signs and superstitions nowadays!"

The operator threw a switch on the instrument board and pointed his hand instinctively on the key, ready to begin sending the message. Then he grinned up at Hazard.

"You get to be pretty much of an old sea dog after you have crossed the Atlantic a hundred times," he said. "I've only been on this run two years, but I'm beginning to believe that there is something to these superstitions, crazy as they may sound. Darned if they don't generally work out."

Hazard had almost reached the door; he turned back now with sudden interest.

"Just what superstitions are you referring to?" he asked.

"Well," said the operator with his hands still pressed on the key, "there's the old gag about carrying a load of stiffs. You can usually count on it that when you've got a cargo of stiffs you're due for rough weather."

Hazard looked a little puzzled.

"Stiffs?" he asked. "Do you mean dead people or is it some kind of fish or a special cargo I never heard of?"

"You got me right the first time, sir," the operator said. "Dead ones, corpses in caskets, being carted over to the other side of the pond."

"And that's what you blame the rough weather on? How many have you got on board?"

"About enough to give us rotten weather all the way across," the operator confided. "There's a half dozen of them, in addition to a guy with a limp and a hunchback."

"Isn't that rather unusual?" Hazard asked. "Six corpses in one voyage?"

The operator shrugged.

"A little unusual," he admitted. "Generally we don't have but one or two if any. I remember one trip that was no picnic. There were five stiffs down in the hold and I never saw a rougher trip in my life. On top of the bad weather, we had two murders."

"Phew!" Hazard whistled. "This ought to be a pleasure jaunt then with six stiffs—and a guy who limps and a hunchback. Incidentally, what effect are they supposed to create?"

"Well, we generally figure that a guy with a limp or a crutch and a hunchback is as much bad luck as one stiff."

"Well," ventured Hazard, "let us hope that the old superstition doesn't hold true."

As he went out, he heard the sputtering of the wireless and

knew the operator was beginning to send his story. It was growing dark; the lights had just been turned on in C deck, the sheltered promenade where heavy glass windows shut out the wind and rain. The gray, depressing light that still remained in the sky outside and the dim electric bulbs glowing overhead made a strange, weird combination.

THE CABIN side of the deck was lined with steamer chairs, but there was only one occupant in the whole line. He was a man, slightly older than Hazard. His lanky form was stretched out in a sort of careless ease.

Hazard eyed the man as he came nearer. It was hard to see in that weird light but he was sure there was something familiar about him. Then he had it. The man's name was Kildare and he was connected with the bureau of investigation at Washington. Val Kildare. That was it. He'd seen him only yesterday in the horrible streets of Chessfield.

Jerry Hazard, with the easy grace of his calling, stopped before Kildare and nodded.

"You're Kildare, aren't you?" he asked in a low voice. "I saw you at Chessfield."

Kildare's eyes had been on him, the newspaperman now realized, ever since he had come in sight. The other never batted an eye. He smiled and nodded.

"You have a good memory," he admitted, "in fact a better one than I have at the moment. Apparently you're not a crook or I'd be able to place you."

The two men laughed.

THE CASE OF THE SIX COFFINS

"That's a compliment," Hazard admitted. "I'm Jerry Hazard, special correspondent for the McNulty Newspaper Syndicate."

"Oh, Hazard," Kildare nodded, holding out his hand. "Surely. I remember. I've heard good things about you. Yes, I remember seeing you at Chessfield. Horrible affair wasn't it? What report did you make of it to your syndicate?"

"I didn't have much more than the bare facts," Hazard answered. "Most ghastly assignment I ever worked on. What do you know about it, Kildare?"

Kildare's eyes narrowed. He hesitated.

"Sorry," Hazard added quickly. "I didn't mean to try blasting into any of your secrets. But I thought that you, as a Federal man—that is I've always supposed you were a Federal man although I must confess that I've never been quite sure."

He stopped and waited for Kildare to carry on the conversation if he wished. But all semblance of that first smile of Kildare's was gone now. He turned his head abruptly and stared out through the rain-spattered window pane across the deck for a long moment. Then, with characteristic suddenness, he swung his head back so that he faced Hazard full.

"Confound it all, yes," he growled. "No use of keeping mum any longer. Val Kildare. Federal agent."

He spat out the last as though it were poison.

Hazard frowned. "You'll pardon me," he murmured, "if I say you don't seem particularly pleased about it."

"Pleased?" Kildare glared. "Why should I be pleased? Why should I be anything but damnably sore?

"I hope you won't think I'm presuming on your good nature,"

he went on more calmly, "If I spill out my troubles to you. But it would be rather a relief to have someone to talk to—someone whom—well, Hazard, I know you've worked with the police before and I'm sure you can be trusted."

The speaker's cold, narrowed eyes were upon Hazard, waiting.

"I'm sure," Hazard hastened, "that you can trust me with anything you wish. And I'll be highly honored to be taken into your confidence, Kildare."

Kildare nodded. "Good." He fished into his inside coat pocket and brought out a cablegram.

"I got it from headquarters this afternoon after finishing the investigation at Chessfield," he said. "You'll imagine how it affected me after having spent hours in that ghastly village. Read it."

Hazard unfolded the paper quickly. The message was:

> YOU ABE HEREBY RELIEVED OF YOUR DUTIES BECAUSE OF YOUR CONTINUED FAILURE IN SPECIAL MISSION.
>
> HOWER.

"But I can't understand it, Kildare," he exploded as he handed the message back.

Kildare studied him for a minute with his keen, unwavering gray eyes, then spoke in a lowered voice.

"Do you know what special job I was taken from?" he asked.

"No, I don't," Hazard replied. "I've lost track of your work lately, and I haven't seen your name in the newspapers in quite some time."

"That's perfectly natural," Kildare agreed. "I have taken special pains to keep out of the news. Some time ago, I was detailed on the trail of the most dangerous man in the world."

Hazard's eyes widened.

"Good Lord!" he gasped. "You don't mean Wu Fang?"

"Exactly," Kildare nodded. "I've been riding him from pillar to post and he's been riding me as well. The department has been riding me, too, for not getting anything done. You see, that was part of my game, keeping things that I did and learned a secret from everyone else. This Chinese devil has his agents in every part of the world. In fact, I have recently been led to believe that one of his agents is actually working in our headquarters office as a Federal agent."

Kildare smiled rather sadly and shrugged.

"You see," he went on, "why I have not been turning in reports. One day I discovered that Wu Fang, through some mysterious channel, had learned all my plans. The only way he could have received the information was through Federal headquarters. So from then on, I stopped my reports completely. So now I'm out of the department, clean. I'm fired. Oh, it's my own fault, I grant you. But then I acted in the way that I thought best."

Hazard shook his head slowly in a sad negative.

"It's rotten treatment, Kildare," he said. "Something ought to be done about it. What do you intend to do?"

KILDARE GLANCED around before he spoke again. Outside, over the storm-tossed ocean, it was dark now. The rain made a harsh, spattering sound as it licked the window panes in front of them. Now and then a breeze got past the retention windows and came whistling up the closed deck from openings in the stern; it drove icily through their clothing to the very skin.

Kildare waited until he was sure there was no one within earshot before answering Hazard's question.

"I'm going to ride this yellow devil on my own hook," he said slowly. "Either I'm going to get him or he's going to get me before we're through."

Hazard's eyes lighted with admiration.

"By George!" he exclaimed. "That's what I had expected you to say. I've heard a lot about you and I want you to know this. I'm only one man and not a very clever one at that. I'm just a news hound, but if I can give you a hand at any time, I will be only too glad to do so."

Kildare smiled slightly.

"Thanks, Hazard," he said. "Mighty nice of you to say that. Of course, you're joking about being 'only a news hound.' You've done some damned fine work. The way you cut open that McDanold case a year ago was a nice piece of business."

The lanky newspaperman showed a trace of embarrassment.

"Oh, that," he said. "That was just luck. In digging around for news, I stumbled on something the police hadn't found. But—" He broke off abruptly.

He had been staring out of the heavy glass windows into the night. But now, for some reason, his head had turned and he saw a young woman approaching.

She was walking unsteadily, with her hand on the rail to guide her. She wore a dark, silken wrap which the draft, blowing

24

up the deck from the stern, made to cling tightly about her slim figure.

It was that first glimpse of the girl that had caused Hazard to straighten. His eyes never left her face as she came nearer. Even in the light that was shed from the dim bulbs, her beauty was apparent.

"Kildare," he whispered. "Look! Forward there, up the deck. Did you ever see anything as lovely?"

Kildare turned his head, stared.

"Yes," he agreed, "she is beautiful."

The girl didn't seem to notice them. She was having her own troubles in walking along the deck that pushed and heaved with the rolling of the stormy sea.

Somehow Hazard got hold of himself. He couldn't sit bolt upright and stare at the girl as she passed; but just the same his eyes never left her. Even as she went by she didn't seem to have noticed the two men.

"Lord," Hazard breathed, "I didn't know there was such a beautiful girl in the world. Where do you suppose she came from?"

Kildare shrugged. "No telling," he said. He was watching the girl himself.

She disappeared around the end of the deck. As she did so, Hazard was bolt upright again, watching the blank, dim space where the girl had last been. He was breathing a little faster than usual.

Kildare swung his legs off the chair and glanced at his wristwatch.

"It's about time to eat," he ventured. "Feel like eating, Hazard?"

Hazard nodded vacantly. Then suddenly he came to himself.

"Oh," he laughed rather sheepishly. "Sure. I think it will stay down O.K. Shall we go into the dining room?"

The voyage was taking on a new interest for him.

The two men got up; Kildare swung his raincoat over his arm.

"Mind if I wash up first?" he asked. "We'll go in the side door right here. My deck chair is right under my cabin window, you see. I had it arranged that way purposely."

But they had walked no more than a few steps toward the door then both men stopped, stock still. A cry had come from the stern of the ship, a piercing scream of terror, high-pitched and vibrant in the whistling wind.

"What was that?" Kildare barked.

Hazard was already running on wobbly legs over toward the stern.

"The girl," he yelled. "Something has happened to her."

He raced on at top speed, Kildare two paces behind. They reached the stern, just in time to view a sight that chilled Hazard's blood.

The wind was tearing across the deck. It was whipping the silken fabric of the young woman's wrap about her mercilessly. And against the rail, just a few feet from her, crouched a figure so horrible it might have been evil incarnate. Half naked, his bare, dark skin was glistening wet. Before Jerry could move, this dreadful figure leaped forward, grabbed the girl under the armpits and started dragging her across the deck.

Kildare barked out a command—"Stop! Stop, or I'll shoot!"

Out of the tail of his eye, Hazard saw a gun gleam in Kildare's hand. Then the naked man suddenly dropped the girl, leaped for the rail and disappeared over the stern.

Kildare's gun barked out in the darkness. Hazard caught the girl just as she was falling. Throwing his arms around her, he held her up while Kildare leaped for the rail over which the weird, naked figure had dropped. Hazard heard his quick order.

"Take care of the girl," he commanded. "I'm going below."

Then Val Kildare was gone.

CHAPTER 3
MYSTERY GIRL

JERRY HAZARD was aware of some strange emotion quickening him. He knew little else except that the warm, trembling body of the loveliest girl he had ever seen was pressed close to his own. He scarcely heard the sounds of running feet as members of the crew and passengers raced aft in answer to the screams that had sounded a moment before.

Bravely, the young woman seemed to struggle back to consciousness. She straightened with great effort. Her head turned and in the darkness of the after deck, with the wind and the rain lashing about them, she fixed her lovely eyes on him; there was intense fear in them.

Frantically she tried to push him away. Hazard released her until it looked as though she were going to faint, then clasped her again.

27

Her dark, fragrant hair was down, just touching her shoulders. For a second it brushed against his cheek. Then she went limp and her head dropped on Hazard's shoulder. A moment later she spoke.

Her words came in perfect English with the faintest tinge of a foreign accent.

"Who are you, please, and what has happened?"

Jerry Hazard was a young man of the world. He had traveled widely, had been subjected to experiences encountered only by international newspaper correspondents. But now, he was stuttering and stammering for words like a schoolboy in his first fit of puppy love.

"My—my name? Oh, yes. My name is Hazard, Jerry Hazard. You are quite all right with me."

He heard her breathe a sigh of relief.

"Oh, thank you," she said. "Thank you so much."

A group of running passengers and members of the crew were rushing out on the deck.

Now, for the first time, the girl seemed to realize that her head was on his shoulder. She lifted it and stared at him again.

"You—you are of the police?" she asked.

Her words were very calm, but in the darkness, with her face so dose to him, Jerry Hazard thought that a look of fright had come into her eyes again.

"No," he assured quickly. "I'm just a news hound."

Then he forced himself to smile to reassure her.

There was a barrage of questions from the group of passengers, crew, deck hands, and stewards that had by this time reached them. Just as Hazard was about to answer, a first officer pushed through the crowd.

He did some very fast thinking before he replied to that officer's stream of inquiries. He still held the young woman lightly by the arm in case she should grow faint again. He wished Kildare were there to answer these questions; perhaps there was some reason why the circumstances should not be broadcast.

Before he could decide what to say the girl spoke.

"I—I don't remember very much," she said. "I'm so sorry. I guess I was a little silly. I was taking a walk around the enclosed promenade and when I reached the open rear deck something terrified me. As I remember, I became suddenly afraid of being hurled into the sea. You see, there was nothing except a low rail to protect me."

Hazard nodded quickly.

"We found her here," he explained, "trying to keep from falling. I managed to catch her just as she was about to faint."

The young woman nodded.

"That is right, officer," she said. "It's really terrifying out here, isn't it? It's so black."

The first officer turned quickly to a stewardess.

"Take charge of her," he commanded. "I'll send the ship doctor to look her over. What is the number of your stateroom, madam?"

The young woman hesitated for a moment. "Two fifty-two," she said slowly.

Hazard accompanied her to her stateroom and said good-by

Just a few feet from her crouched a figure so horrible
it might have been Evil incarnate.

at the door. Again he thought the eyes of the young woman showed traces of fear, but there was also a remarkable stalwartness about her, a surprising ability to choke back the terror that must have followed such an experience.

"I can not thank you enough, Mr. Hazard," she said.

Then, in a voice so low that only he could hear—"I am sure I can trust you."

For a fleeting moment, she laid her hand on his arm.

Hazard bowed. "You may be sure of that."

THE CASE OF THE SIX COFFINS

The girl forced a smile.

"Good night and thank you again," she said.

"Good night."

The door was closed. Hazard lingered there for a moment, staring at the shut portal. Then he turned and walked down the corridor, hardly realizing that he was holding fast to the silken rope along the rail to steady himself against the roll of the ship. He was moving like a man in a fog.

A LITTLE way down the corridor, he met Kildare coming up. The government man's eyes were narrowed and questioning.

"Did you find it?" Hazard whispered. "The half-naked thing?"

Kildare shook his head.

"I found nothing," he said shortly. "What happened to the girl? Is she in her state-room?"

"Yes," Hazard nodded. "A stewardess is with her and one of the ship officers is sending the doctor in to have a look at her."

"Did you tell them about the naked man?"

Hazard shook his head.

"No, she—I mean, I thought perhaps it wasn't necessary."

The other eyed him strangely. When he spoke again his whispered voice was a little crisper.

"You started to say something about the girl, Hazard. What was it?"

Hazard shifted his eyes instantly.

"Well, confound it all, Kildare," he blurted out, "the thing seemed so strange. The girl didn't want it known, either."

Kildare's expression never changed.

"Go on," he said.

"It was nothing," Hazard assured him, "except this: The ship officer was plying me with questions and I was thinking like the very devil, trying to decide whether I should tell him everything or not. I had just decided to say nothing about it when she came to the rescue. She said she was frightened by the pitching of the ship. I made my story match with hers."

"Good!" nodded Kildare. "No need of the passengers and crew getting panicky about things that are going to happen on this voyage. Also I would just as soon do things my own way without interference."

"But look here," Hazard said. "I haven't been able to figure this girl out yet. Why do you suppose she wanted the attack kept secret?"

"I don't know. That's one of the things we've got to find out. Don't talk any more now. Here comes the room steward." He raised his voice. "Just a moment, steward!"

Reaching into his pocket, he drew out a bill.

"What room?" he asked Hazard.

"Two fifty-two."

Kildare turned to the newcomer.

"You are the room steward for two fifty-two?" he asked.

The steward bowed. "Yes, sir."

Kildare flashed the badge inside his coat. When the steward looked properly impressed, he slipped the bill into his hand.

"Keep close watch on that room. I'm in two seventy-three on the other side of the ship. Tell me about anything that goes on, will you?"

"Yes, sir." The steward nodded, took the bill and started to move on.

"And steward," Kildare added, "remember this is between you and me. Say nothing to anyone else on the ship about it."

"Yes, sir," the steward promised and walked on down the corridor.

"Come, Hazard," Kildare suggested. "Let's go down to my room as we were planning to do in the first place. We'll clean up a bit and have dinner together—if you still feel like eating."

A few moments later Val Kildare was inserting a key in the lock of his cabin. He turned it, tried the knob; turned it the other way.

"That's funny," he said. "I locked my door when I went out. Now it's unlocked. Maybe the steward was cleaning up and forgot to lock it."

He pushed the door open—then stood to stare in astonishment. The contents of the cabin were turned completely upside down. The bed clothing of both upper and lower bunks was rumpled and dumped on the floor. Two traveling bags were open and their contents spilled all over. His two extra suits and a top coat were lying on the bare mattress.

For a moment his eyes blazed. Then he nodded slowly.

"I might have known it," he groaned. "The whole affair was merely a decoy."

Hazard looked at him with a puzzled expression.

"I don't see what you mean, Kildare."

"I mean that scream and all the rest of it," Kildare explained. "It was a plant to get me far enough away from this room so

34

that it could be searched."

"But," objected Hazard. "Why couldn't they have searched it while you were sitting out on deck?"

Kildare smiled. "There's one thing you forget. My chair is placed directly

Val Kildare

under this window and I left the window open inside the blinds so that I could hear any sound. Apparently, they didn't dare take a chance of searching the room while I was directly outside."

"But who would do such—" Hazard began.

Kildare smiled again, ever so slightly.

"One of Wu Fang's agents," he said calmly. "They are the only ones who might be interested."

Hazard gulped. "But what would they be looking for? I can understand why they might try to kill you; but have you something special that they want?"

"There is a little matter of a half-torn note that is probably behind it all," Kildare replied. "I'll tell you about it later. You may as well wash first, Hazard. I'll make up the bunks again and straighten the room while you're doing that. No use calling in the room steward. The fewer people who know about this, the freer we'll be to work as we see fit."

JERRY HAZARD was growing more and more perplexed about a number of things, but particularly about the dark, mysterious beauty and the part she might be playing in Wu Fang's schemes. He pondered the problem for some time and it wasn't until they sat in the dining saloon at dinner that he asked the question which was uppermost in his mind.

"Why would a marvelous creature like that be teamed up with Wu Fang? I can't believe it."

"Ssshh." Kildare cautioned. "We'll find out more as soon as we finish dinner."

Jerry lapsed into silence and finished his meal hurriedly. He couldn't keep his glance from roving about the dining room in the hope that the young woman would come in; but when they finally rose and left, he had seen nothing of her.

"I'm going up to the wireless room for a few minutes," Kildare said. "Better come with me. I'm going to telegraph Scotland Yard. They are in closer touch with Wu Fang and his operations than I am and might know of some hook-up."

A new operator, the night man, was on duty. Kildare took a radio blank and, standing so that Hazard could read over his shoulder, began writing swiftly.

GIRL ABOUT TWENTY. DARK EYES AND HAIR.
BEAUTIFUL. ABOUT FIVE FEET SIX. NAME MOHRA.
ADVISE IF CONNECTED WITH W.F.
KILDARE.

"How do you know her name?" Hazard demanded.

Kildare smiled.

"You wouldn't make much of a detective," he laughed. "Oh, I know the girl's got you all bottled up so that you can't think of anything else. I simply went down and described her to the purser."

"But is that her only name?"

Kildare shrugged. "So far as I know."

He turned the message around and passed it to the operator, who read the first line, then looked up quickly.

"Oh, Scotland Yard, sir," he said in a voice. "Here's a message that just came in."

He passed it across the counter. Kildare frowned as he read it.

GEORGE GREGORY SS BERGENLAND SUSPECT-
ED W. F. AND AGENTS ON BERGENLAND BOUND
NEW YORK.
CHIEF INSPECTOR SCOTLAND YARD.

They finished reading it just as the operator reached the end of Kildare's message, saw the signature. He jumped.

"You—you are not Mr. Gregory of Scotland Yard?" he stammered.

Kildare shook his head. "No."

Then he smiled as the operator snatched back the radiogram.

"Excuse me, sir. I'm sorry for the error. I hope no harm has been done."

"On the contrary," Kildare laughed. "I'm glad I saw the

message. You see, I have been working with Scotland Yard. Just keep the whole thing to yourself and no harm will come of it."

"Yes, sir," nodded the operator, plainly flustered. "You see, sir, I thought you were Mr. Gregory because you were sending a message to Scotland Yard."

"Forget it," advised Kildare, "and get my message off as quickly as possible, will you?"

The operator nodded, threw a switch and grabbed a key.

They walked out to the deck, into the cold, biting wind and rain without a word; but the moment they were in the lounge, Hazard turned to the secret service man.

"Do you suppose that Wu Fang and his agents are really on this ship?"

Kildare nodded. "I suspected it before. Now I'm positive of it. Wu Fang is on The Bergenland."

CHAPTER 4
SCOTLAND YARD MAN

JERRY HAZARD was aware of a cold chill racing up his spine at the thought of being on the same ship with Wu Fang.

"Good Lord!" he gasped. "That means almost anything is apt to happen before we reach New York."

Kildare shrugged.

"There's no use getting panicky about it. Let's get a table in the corner of the bar and have an after-dinner whiskey and soda and a smoke. What do you say?"

Hazard nodded and they walked aft.

"You were covering that Chessfield tragedy. Let's get back to that," Kildare said after they were seated in the bar. "What do you make of it?"

"It's the most mysterious thing I ever heard of. No one but a fiend could have perpetrated it."

"No one but Wu Fang," Kildare corrected.

"You think Wu Fang was behind it?" Hazard asked.

Kildare nodded. "I am sure of it," he asserted.

"Good Lord!" The newspaperman sat up straight. "That's the best part of the story. Have I your permission to radio this information to my syndicate?"

Kildare's left hand flashed out and fell in a restraining manner on Hazard's arm.

"Wait a minute, old man," he said. "Not so fast please. I have a hunch I can work on Wu Fang better with less red tape and restraint. And I hope that he believes that I'm fired, and have given up in disgust."

"O.K.," Hazard agreed. "I'll say nothing to the syndicate about you. But what makes you so sure that Wu Fang is responsible?"

"In the first place," Kildare said, "there's no other man on the face of the earth who would so such a thing. In the second place, I traced the affair from the docks of New York about a week ago to Chessfield the other night. Have you ever heard of a young inventor by the name of George Opporte?"

Hazard thought for a moment.

"Why, yes," he said. "Didn't he invent a mysterious gas recently? There was a story in all the papers."

"Exactly," Kildare nodded. "The gas was mentioned for the Darien prize, which, as you know, is awarded each year for the newest, most deadly instrument of war. I was sure that one of Wu Fang's agents would be after it and advised the police to keep a careful watch on George Opporte. But something slipped and a bottle of the liquid was stolen from his laboratory. I traced it to The Utopia and cornered Wu Fang's agent just as he was going up the gang-plank. He threw the bottle into the water. Someone—I couldn't see him very well in the dark—dived over after it. That's the last I saw of it or the diver. The ship sailed on schedule that night. I killed Wu Fang's agent and I also got part of a message which was wrapped around the bottle. Here it is."

He handed Hazard a crumpled piece of torn paper.

"You see," he explained, "I imagine Wu Fang has received the bottle and the other half of this message. The note is in code, except for Opporte's name. You can see the last part, 'porte,' at the bottom here."

Hazard stared at the strange figures of the torn note.

"Why," he demanded, "do you keep such a dangerous thing? Why don't you destroy it?"

"For several reasons," Kildare smiled. "I'd give a lot to decipher that code, for one thing. Then, I like to hold something as a possible safeguard to bargain with Wu Fang if he should get me in too tight a spot. You see, I have a hunch Wu Fang wants this bit of writing badly. It is very possible that the agent who stole the gas was acting on his own initiative and that Wu Fang knows nothing of the inventor or the gas itself. In that case, he would need this note to learn the inventor's name—if nothing else."

He sipped at his drink and puffed at a long, slim cigar that he had lighted. Hazard bit his lip.

"But why," he demanded, "should Wu Fang kill the inhabitants of a peaceful little village of Chessfield?"

"Apparently," Kildare told him, "you don't know Wu Fang and his methods as well as I do. He is the most unscrupulous devil I've ever encountered. I believe he killed those people merely to experiment with the contents of the bottle."

"Good Lord!" breathed Hazard. "You mean he didn't have any special grudge against any of them?"

"Exactly," Kildare nodded. "He was simply using human guinea pigs. As a matter of fact, I checked up all airports around London and learned that a plane was chartered the night before the people were murdered."

"What does Scotland Yard think of it?" asked Hazard.

"They're not saying," Kildare said. "I worked with them up to the time I was discharged from service, but they must have learned I was fired because they stopped cooperating since. Perhaps they even suspect me of being in on the plot because I was discharged at the same time. That's why this Scotland Yard man, Gregory, hasn't gotten in touch with me."

THE TWO men sipped their drinks in silence. Jerry Hazard was smoking nervously, lighting one cigarette from another.

At length, he blurted out, "Confound it, Kildare. I still can't believe that a sweet, beautiful girl like Mohra could be mixed up with Wu Fang."

Kildare smiled tolerantly.

"I got some information about Wu Fang a little while ago," he said. "As a matter of fact, I choked it out of one of his agents. It seems that Wu Fang has a large assortment of strange, ghastly and clever agents. Take that fellow who was attacking Mohra tonight on the deck. You can't deny he was a horrible specimen of humanity."

"Yes," Hazard agreed, "and that's what makes me believe that she hasn't anything to do with it—not of her own free will, anyway. Why, that beast was dragging her to the rail. I really think he was going to throw her over into the sea. And how did he get there in the first place without somebody spotting him?"

"By a rope," Kildare said. "You didn't see it, but I did. There was a rope slung double around one of the supports of the rail. All he had to do after he had slid down the rope was to pull one end of it and it would slide free of the post. I saw it vanish into one of the repair hatches under the stern."

"You mean," demanded Hazard, "that he climbed up from the hatch below on that rope and then slid back again and pulled the rope after him?"

"Exactly," Kildare nodded.

"But how in the devil," Hazard objected, "could he have gotten the rope around the post in the first place?"

"It's quite apparent that he didn't," Kildare smiled. "That

dark-eyed beauty of yours might have been carrying it under her cape."

Jerry Hazard flared for a moment.

"Kildare," he snapped, "I don't know whether you're kidding me or whether you're in earnest, but I tell you you're going too far in implicating this girl with Wu Fang."

"Take it easy," Kildare advised. "Don't let love at first sight counteract your common sense. I don't know what the girl's connection with Wu Fang is or I don't know what she is to him. That's none of my business. But I am satisfied that she is working with him, whether she likes it or not."

Chewing the long, slim cigar in the corner of his mouth, he ticked off various items on his fingers as he mentioned them.

"There is her story of taking a walk on the deck. All right. Assume that that was purely an accident, that she didn't intend to draw our attention. I'll grant that she didn't look at us. That in itself is rather suspicious. But let it go at that.

"She reaches the after deck of the ship. She has had time enough after she's passed from our view to draw a rope around a rail post and drop it down to the hatch. Then she screamed and by the time we got there, this half-naked monster was just ready to spring on and drag her to the rail.

"All right, we'll forget that part of it. But did you notice as the half-naked beast ran for the rail that she shielded him from my gun?"

"You're wrong," Hazard flared. "You're absolutely wrong. She swayed with the ship. I saw her. The ship tossed her over to the right."

Kildare shrugged.

"O.K.," he said. "The ship tossed her, and then let's say that the half-naked creature kept her between him and us. I saw him disappear and the rope vanished into the hatch. Then, when the officer came, the girl helped you lie about what actually happened. For some reason, she didn't want the facts known."

"I've been thinking that over," Hazard cut in. "Any nice girl wouldn't want to be mixed up in such a scandal."

"Perhaps," Kildare admitted. "On the other hand, if she were a normal girl, she would be scared green. She would insist on going directly to the captain and telling him about it, and furthermore, she would insist on a guard for the remainder of the voyage.

"Also there is the ransacking of my state-room. After that, we find that a Scotland Yard agent is on board and read a message advising him that Wu Fang is on the boat. And don't forget this, Hazard. Wu Fang doesn't venture out alone. When he travels, he always has his cunning agents and deadly creatures with him.

"And here's the last thing I was going to tell you. He has a collection of beautiful women from all parts of the world working for him. I don't know how he gets them. Perhaps he raises them up from children. Maybe he steals them from their parents. But he has them, nevertheless. Mohra might be one."

Jerry Hazard was staring hard at his almost empty glass, staring through it at the table beneath. His jaws were clenched. He was fighting the belief that was slowly growing within him;

he took a fresh cigarette from his pack and lighted it from the half-smoked stub of another.

KIILDARE SLAPPED his shoulder and advised, "Take it easy, old man. She's beautiful, I'll grant you. But it's going to be better if you look things squarely in the face. May save a lot of disappointment later on."

Hazard didn't answer for a long time. At length, he gulped down the remainder of his drink and looked up.

"O.K.," he breathed. "I guess you're right. Have you any idea who among the passengers might be agents of Wu Fang? I mean, have you made any check of the passenger list?"

Kildare shook his head.

"It wouldn't do any good," he said. "There's one check that I do want to make, though—who this Scotland Yard man is."

Hazard jerked his head toward a tall, angular broad-shoul-dered man standing at the bar.

"I've been watching him since we've been sitting here," he said. "He has a table near us at the dining saloon and I remem-ber now that he was one of the first to arrive on the deck when Mohra screamed."

Kildare studied the tall man for a moment.

"He looks the part," he decided. "I noticed him at dinner, too."

Taking a notebook from his pocket, he scribbled on the torn page and then motioned the waiter.

"Boy," he ordered, "take this note to the tall gentleman stand-ing at the bar, will you?"

The waiter bowed, took the note, and approached the bar. A

moment later, they saw the tall man glance at the note, then turn and stare at them. He hesitated, then walked toward them.

Hazard and Kildare stood up to greet him.

"You are Gregory, aren't you?" Kildare asked. "Allow me to introduce myself. I am Val Kildare, former Federal agent and this is Hazard of the McNulty syndicate. Won't you join us?"

Gregory seemed amiable enough. After he had sat down and a round of whiskeys and sodas had been ordered, Kildare continued.

"This voyage smacks of a rather interesting trip with our friend, Wu Fang, on board, doesn't it?"

Gregory eyed him speculatively. Then he smiled.

"Righto," he admitted, "but how did you know?"

"I suspected it after the things that have taken place this evening."

"By George!" said Gregory. "You're a bit keen, what? But what I can't figure is where the blighter and his agents can be hiding."

"This is a pretty large ship," Kildare reminded him. "They have a lot of space in which to hide. Of course, they might not be hiding at all; they may have staterooms like everyone else."

"Speaking of state-rooms," Gregory ventured, "I believe I saw you cross the private corridor to our state-rooms, did I not? It's odd that you should get a stateroom next to mine, isn't it?"

"I didn't see you, but it's odd," Kildare admitted with a touch of sarcasm in his voice. "Much odder that I should get stateroom next to you, not knowing you were on board, than that you should have a state-room next to me under the circumstances."

The Scotland Yard man looked blank for a moment, then he laughed.

"We may as well get the thing over with," he said. "The Yard was a bit suspicious of you, I'm sorry to admit, because of your sudden discharge. Not very suspicious, but enough so that, since I was going to New York, they suggested I keep an eye on you. I thought the best way to do that was to get a room next to yours. I am in two-seventy-four, you know."

"I didn't know it until just now," Kildare admitted, "but I suspected the rest of it."

They talked on during the evening and became quite confidential, despite the slight suspicion cast by Scotland Yard upon Val Kildare. At length, Gregory stifled a yawn, glanced at a heavy gold watch that hung from a gold chain across his vest.

"It's getting late," he said. "We don't know when we're going to sleep on this voyage, so I believe I'll turn in if you gentlemen will excuse me."

The two Americans rose and bowed and Gregory left them. When they were alone Hazard broached the subject that had been in his mind for some time.

"You know, I have been thinking about this sleeping situation. We both have state-rooms alone. You have two bunks in yours. Suppose I move my belongings into your state-room and we ride this thing through together?"

Kildare nodded instantly.

"Good idea," he agreed. "I was about to speak of the same thing myself. How about another one just to top off the evening?"

"Right," Hazard nodded.

Perhaps ten minutes had elapsed since Gregory had gone when they rose and made their way, rather unsteadily, to Hazard's state-room. Together, they collected the correspondent's baggage, and lugged it below. They were about two hundred feet from the little corridor that connected the inner rooms designated to Kildare and Gregory. Suddenly, Kildare stopped short.

"Look!" he gasped. "Someone is coming from my hallway!"

Hazard froze.

CHAPTER 5
A CRY FOR HELP

THE FIGURE of the man was hard to describe as he darted out of the passage and into the main corridor. He must have sighted the two men at the same instant they saw him because he whirled quickly before they could get a look at his face. Walking in such a position that they couldn't tell whether he was tall or short, he moved ahead at a fast gait.

Kildare started chasing him at top speed.

"Stop! Stop! Or I'll shoot!"

Hazard, also, dropped his bags and broke into a wild run behind Kildare. The next thing they knew, the man had vanished into a passage on the left.

"Go back and watch your bags," Kildare called out over his shoulder. "I'll meet you at the door of my state-room."

"But—" Hazard protested.

"Do as I say," snapped Kildare.

Then, as Hazard stopped and turned back, Kildare dashed into the same corridor that had swallowed the fleeing figure.

Five minutes later, he returned to Hazard, who was waiting with his luggage in front of the door of state-room 273.

"Find him?" Hazard asked.

The other shook his head.

"No. The night and the dark hallway swallowed him up. Confound it, I didn't even get a good look at him."

As he spoke he began to pound frantically on Gregory's door. A moment later a strange look spread over his face. There were sounds of life and movement behind the door of 274. Then the door opened and Gregory stood silhouetted in the light of his room behind him. He had his shirt off and was in his stocking feet.

"Oh, I say." He smiled, then stopped as he saw the blank expression on Kildare's face. "Has something gone wrong?"

Kildare took a long breath.

"No," he said. "Apparently not. I was afraid you were dead, Gregory."

"Dead?" echoed Gregory as though he were not sure he had heard correctly. "Dead? Oh. I say. I can't imagine. What put such an idea in your head, Kildare?"

Hazard saw Kildare bite his lip, turn to go.

"I'm sorry to bother you, Gregory," he said. "Perhaps he was searching my room again."

Gregory looked puzzled for a moment, then his eyes widened.

"Oh, I say, you must mean the chap that just left my room."

"Then he *was* in your room?" Kildare demanded with apparent relief.

"Yes. Yes, indeed. A chap who used to be with Scotland Yard years ago. Not one of the inspectors, of course. He was an office boy in my department. He chanced to be on board and dropped in to see me. As a matter of fact, he was just knocking on my door when I arrived after leaving you gentlemen."

"What's his name?" Kildare asked.

"Name?" repeated Gregory vacantly. "Let's see. Why, confound it, we always called him Jimmy. That's all I can remember. I called him Jimmy tonight."

"You're sure you recognize him?" Kildare probed.

"Why, of course." The Scotland Yard man laughed. "I say, you're getting all worked up about this thing, old man. Of course I know him. As I say, I haven't seen him in quite a number of years. He was a little fellow when he worked in my department. He has grown up now; years at that stage of life make quite a few changes in a man. And now you must excuse me. I want to get a bit of sleep."

Kildare hesitated for only a moment. Then he gave a short nod.

"O.K.," he said. "I just wanted to make sure. Good night."

Gregory closed the door. Kildare unlocked his own, but he didn't usher Hazard in first. Instead, he told him to wait outside.

"I want to take a look around before you come in," he said. "Pick up that small suitcase of yours and hold it ready. If anything tries to escape from this room, for the love of heaven, kill it."

Hazard frowned and his brows knit together as he stared at Kildare.

"Kill it?" he asked in a low voice. "Kill what? What the devil are you driving at, Kildare? Is something getting under your hide?"

Without turning, Kildare snapped savagely, "Do as I say."

He pushed the door in cautiously, stepped across the threshold.

Hazard raised the small suitcase, ready to strike as he had been ordered. He saw Kildare walk to a corner and pick up a cane. With the cane, he pulled the belongings out of his grips, pulled clothing down from their hooks on the wall.

Next, he turned to the bunks and, still using the cane, plucked the clothing from the beds. He shook it well and deposited it on the floor.

Hazard remained standing at the door. The hair along his spine seemed to be rising. He didn't know why, but there was a curious, prickly feeling all the way down his back. Perhaps it was watching Kildare work with that cane as though something ghastly, something deadly, might leap out at him. He tried to calm himself.

"Look here, Kildare," he said softly. "I'm a bit thick on this. You just made up those bunks a few hours ago and now you're tearing them apart again."

Kildare gave a short nod. Suddenly he jumped and turned, the cane upraised. His eyes seemed to be bulging a little as they stared at the lower edge of the room opposite the bunks where the wall and the floor joined. He took one or two stealthy steps forward.

"Get it if it comes out," he said softly.

The next instant he straightened and shook himself.

"It must have been a shadow," he muttered.

Hazard set his lips grimly and stepped into the room.

"Listen, Kildare, you're acting like a madman. Next thing, you'll be telling me you're Napoleon."

"If Wu Fang strikes," Kildare retorted, "you'll wish you were Napoleon."

As he spoke he turned. His eyes snapped as he saw Hazard standing inside the door, suitcase dropped. His teeth drew back in a snarl of rage.

"Damn it," he fairly hissed. "I thought I told you to stand outside the door and strike anything that came out with that suitcase. Either do that or get back to your room and forget this."

There was something powerful and compelling about Val Kildare in a rage. Hazard obeyed without another question. He was tense now, tense as a finely-tuned string of gut. This was important, ghastly important. He didn't understand why, but Kildare knew Wu Fang and his methods. He expected something.

PERHAPS TEN minutes passed while Kildare went through the room again from top to bottom, from wall to wall, lifting clothes with the cane, shaking them, searching into folds of the bed clothes that he might have missed before. At length, his shoulders drooped and he took a long breath.

"O.K., Hazard," he said. "Come in. I guess I was wrong—wrong about this room, at least. Here, let me help with that luggage."

Then, when Hazard and his luggage were inside, Kildare locked and bolted the door. Suddenly, he dropped to his knees and eyed the crack under the door. He shook his head.

"There isn't a quarter of an inch of space there," he said. "I don't believe anything could get in through that."

He rose, dropped limply into a chair and stared at the wall opposite.

"No," he said, shaking his head slowly back and forth. "I guess I was wrong about this room. Heaven knows, I hope so."

"Just what," Hazard demanded, "were you looking for?"

Kildare turned his head slowly until his narrowed eyes fell upon Jerry Hazard's face.

"You remember, Hazard," he began, "I told you in the bar that Wu Fang has many kinds of horrible assistants. Well, they are not all human."

"But what made you suspicious just now?"

"The way that supposedly former office boy ran when he saw us convinces me that he was one of Wu Fang's agents. I believe he had us marked for killing tonight, but it so happened that Gregory surprised him in the corridor just as he was entering our room. He had a good story cooked up about being a former office boy in Scotland Yard. Perhaps he was. I thought at first

53

he'd gotten Gregory, then I thought of the other angle—our room."

"But Kildare," Hazard objected, "why should you tear up the whole room, dump the bed clothing off the bunks and all that sort of thing? And to top it all off, you did it with a cane as though you were afraid to touch anything with your hands."

"You say that," Kildare answered, "because you don't know Wu Fang as well as I do. He doesn't kill like another murderer might, by running up and sticking a knife in your back or shooting you. I learned from his agent that he has a breeding farm. The agent didn't know where it was. Lord knows I'd like to find out. At any rate, on this farm, he raises every conceivable kind of poisonous beast. You don't know when you are going to be attacked by Wu Fang or how it's going to be done."

Hazard looked grave and nodded now with a little more understanding.

"I see," he said. "Then you figure that Jimmy might have let something in our room—perhaps some poisonous little beast that might be hiding in the folds of your clothing, waiting for a chance to strike?"

"Yes," Kildare nodded. "That's it."

The two men began to rearrange the cabin now. Hazard had scoffed at Kildare's caution a few minutes before, but now that he realized the full danger, he handled everything with merely his fingertips. His nerves were on edge. He was ready to jump back at any movement. His eyes were glued constantly to the materials that he touched.

Once, he let go of a sheet with a gasp and darted back. The

thing had seemed to move a short way from where he clutched it. Then it lay flat and he was hopeful, if not too sure, that it was merely a pocket of air underneath the fold.

A little later, hoping that some explanation from Kildare would quiet his nerves, he sat down on the made-up bunk and eyed the Federal man speculatively.

"Listen, Kildare," he argued, "how could that fellow have placed anything in our room? The door was locked, for one thing."

"How do you think," Kildare demanded, "that the stewards get in? They have pass keys, of course."

"Yes, yes, I know," Hazard added hurriedly, "but what I'm thinking is this: Assuming that Gregory surprised the man before he could enter our room, how could he have slipped anything in here?"

Kildare didn't answer. He was sitting in the single straight-back chair the cabin afforded, studying the pattern in the carpet. Finally, he looked up, shrugged.

"Oh, come," he said. "Let's try to forget it. We've searched thoroughly high and low and haven't found a thing that would warrant nourishing any suspicions. Perhaps I've gotten both of us worked up over nothing. Let's assume that the fellow was merely an innocent visitor."

Then his eyes hardened. He shook his head stubbornly.

"No, confound it," he said. "We can't do that. The fellow ran, didn't he? Well, anyway—"

He stood up and yawned. "Let's turn in," he suggested, "and get what sleep we can."

They turned in, but Jerry Hazard could not shut his eyes. He lay in the upper berth, tossing restlessly. The sea was rolling worse than ever. It must be past midnight by now, maybe two o'clock.

MINUTES DRAGGED by like hours. There was a constant, ever-increasing brain torture, working him up to a high, nervous tension. The room was pitch-dark except for a very dim light that filtered through the slanting blinds. The window beyond the blinds was securely locked. Kildare had insisted on that, and Hazard had readily agreed.

The atmosphere inside the cabin was growing more and more stuffy. Perhaps that helped cause those things to appear before his wide eyes. Once, he thought he saw something hanging from the paneled ceiling directly above him, something that weaved back and forth ever so slightly.

He lay still, frozen with panic, for what seemed an eternity of time, watching, watching. He tried to decide whether it was a living thing or a figment of his own half-insane fancy.

Then, suddenly, he heard a slight, hissing sound close by. Mustering his courage, he brought his right arm out of the bed clothing and struck at the shadows overhead, ducking to the outside of the bunk as he did so. He missed and struck again. His arm was truer that time, but there was nothing there. A trick of shadow, perhaps, played by the very dim light.

Then, as he lay there, gasping, over the edge of the bunk, he realized what the hissing sound was. It was the measured breathing of Kildare in the lower bunk. Val Kildare was sound asleep.

That, in itself, did more to shatter Hazard's tortured nerves than anything else. It gave him a feeling of aloneness, as though he had been cast into a chamber of horror with a comrade who had promptly vanished, leaving him to face the menace in solitary terror.

Hazard forced himself back in the bunk, slammed his head back on the pillow.

He mumbled to himself, "Come on, Hazard. You'll go crazy at this rate before long. It's all imagination. You've got to get some sleep. There's nothing in here."

He shut his eyes with a great effort. He must sleep. What could he do to induce slumber? Count sheep. That was it. He forced into his mind the vision of sheep passing through a narrow niche in a stone wall. One, two, three, four, five.

What was the matter with that sixth sheep? It had funny-looking wool on it. The wool seemed to wriggle. They were snakes, millions of them, that covered that sheep's hide instead of wool. And the other sheep were all the same—six, seven, eight.

He was breaking out in a cold sweat, but he forced his eyes to remain shut. Nine, ten. He tried to make his imagination turn those sheep with their hides of tiny, crawling snakes back into normal sheep with coats of white wool. But he couldn't.

The snakes on the tenth sheep began to leave the animal's body. They crawled out in a great horde, swarming over the ground. Tiny snakes with pointed noses and wide heads; they came straight for him. Now they were all about him. He turned and tried to run, but his feet seemed glued to the ground.

Then suddenly something worse happened. The thirteenth sheep was just passing through the opening in the wall—and it had a human face. It was a familiar face. It wasn't Kildare; it was—he couldn't quite identify it. The mouth of the human face on the thirteenth sheep opened and a blood-curdling cry emitted.

"Help! Help!"

Jerry Hazard awoke with a start. The sheets were wet with sweat. He gasped and blinked. Thank heaven it had been only a dream. He must have fallen asleep while counting the fifth sheep.

No, it wasn't a dream. He was wide awake now. And there was that cry again—a ghastly, piercing cry. It rang through the cabin and the ship. It struck terror to Jerry Hazard in the dark of the night and chilled his blood.

He jerked up straight in the upper bunk with such suddenness that his head slammed against the ceiling. The blow stunned him for a moment, but he was moving instinctively, sliding off the edge toward the floor.

His legs came in contact with another figure. Strong arms grasped him, then he was being hurled against the opposite wall of the cabin. The blow stunned him again for an instant.

A light went on, flooding the room with its illumination. He saw Val Kildare staring at him wildly.

"What is it?" he rasped. "I heard a cry for help. Sorry I grappled with you. Are you O.K.?"

Hazard nodded.

"Listen!" he hissed.

Mohra

From the partition against which Kildare had thrown him, they heard sounds of wild threshing.

"Quick!" Kildare snapped. "Gregory!"

They both rushed for the door and as they threw it open, the cry came again.

"Help! Help!"

It was now a high-pitched scream of terror. At the same time, oddly enough, there was a strange, nasal note in the sound.

Hazard and Kildare, clad in their pajamas, rushed out into the little corridor. As they reached Gregory's door, the cry died away in a strangled, gurgling sound. Then there was a thud as of a heavy body falling.

Kildare was turning the doorknob, pushing on the door.

"It's locked," he groaned.

As he said that, he drew back and Hazard joined him. Together, they charged the door. There was a crash as the portal gave. Kildare caught himself and grabbed Hazard.

"Don't fall, for the love of heaven," he gasped. "Damn! Where's the light switch? There! I have it."

A bright glow illuminated the small room. Kildare gave a warning cry.

"Look out!"

CHAPTER 6
THE SHADOW KILLER

HAZARD LEAPED aside, back into the hallway, as Kildare uttered the warning. He didn't know what he was being warned against, but he saw Kildare grasp the top of the door that was partly open and pull himself up against it as though he were chinning himself on a horizontal bar.

The light in the corridor was dim, but in it Kildare saw something. It was a flashing shadow, indistinct and moving too fast along the junction of the wall and floor to be distinguished plainly. It was something that ran or crawled with lightning speed from Gregory's room.

As it sped away, Kildare dropped to the floor.

"Follow it! Follow that thing! I'll be along."

Hazard whirled from the private hallway and into the main corridor. Kildare tarried only long enough to rush into his cabin, grab the cane, then he followed. But though Hazard in the lead, ran at top speed, the thing was getting away from him. Even now, out in the bright light of the main corridor, it was moving so fast he couldn't tell what it was.

He reached the main stairway just in time to see it slither between the spindles and drop into the stairwell below. Then he was plunging headlong down the steps in pursuit, with Kildare after him. They searched frantically below. After a few moments Kildare uttered a curse.

"It's gone," he said. "Let's get back to Gregory's room."

They ran back and Kildare pushed open the door of 274 a little farther. Something was lying against it, a heavy body. Reaching in, he shoved the body back so that he could squeeze past.

The Scotland Yard man lay face downward. Kildare turned him over on his back. There was a slight ooze of blood at the nose and a dust mark from the carpet on the tip of it that showed where it had struck as he fell.

There were no other apparent signs of injury. Carefully, Kildare slipped his hand inside Gregory's pajamas, felt the heart. He gave a short nod.

"Dead," he said shortly, "as I expected."

They heard the sound of running feet in the corridor. Then

the room steward burst in. Behind him came several of the crew and the second officer.

Kildare stood up beside the still form.

"This is Gregory," he told the second officer, "George Gregory of Scotland Yard. He has been murdered."

"Good heavens!" gasped the officer. "Do you know who killed him?"

Kildare shook his head.

"I think he was poisoned," he ventured. "We saw something running from the room when we burst in. It was a small animal—perhaps a snake."

The second officer's face went white. By this time the whole hallway was rapidly filling with white-faced passengers.

"I think," Kildare suggested in a low voice, "it would be just as well if you ordered everyone to their state-rooms for the rest of the night. You're going to have a very nervous group of passengers on your hands if you let them hang around here."

The second officer nodded quickly. "Good idea."

He issued the orders and the passengers were hurried back to their state-rooms. Then he dispatched the steward for the doctor.

The medical man arrived in a few moments and made a quick examination.

"He is dead, isn't he, doctor?" Kildare asked.

The doctor looked up perplexed. "He's not only dead, but as stiff as a ramrod already. You say you think its poison?"

Kildare nodded. "A small animal escaped just as we burst

into the room. Perhaps a poisonous snake that slipped on board at a tropical port recently."

The doctor looked more puzzled than before.

"But," he protested, "we haven't stopped in a tropical port for at least three months."

"That's what puzzled me," chimed in the second officer. "We've been sailing between England and New York for three months."

"The snake might have come on board before that," Kildare ventured. "At least, one guess is just as good as another."

He helped the doctor strip the pajamas from the dead body and watched him make a careful examination for wounds. As the examination proceeded, it was Val Kildare's turn to look puzzled.

"That's a very peculiar thing," the doctor said at length. "I can't find a single wound on this man to indicate he was bitten by a poisonous animal. There's only this little blood from his nose, and from your description of the way you found him, I should say that was caused when he fell face down on the floor."

Suddenly, an idea flashed into Jerry Hazard's mind. He glanced at Kildare and hesitated for a moment, but Kildare's perplexity seemed genuine.

"Look," Jerry said. "Supposing his nose didn't bleed when he bumped it?"

"Oh, but it certainly did," the doctor argued.

Kildare was staring at Jerry, an interested gleam in his eye.

"I'm beginning to see what you mean, Hazard," he said. "Go ahead."

"Well, you see," Hazard continued, "Kildare and I were awakened out of a sound sleep by Gregory's cry for help. We got to him as quickly as possible, but he fell before we could break open his door. The last time he screamed, there was a nasal tone in his voice. I don't know how to express it exactly except that it was as though he might be holding his nose or as though something had gotten into the nasal passages."

"Great Scott!" the doctor exclaimed. "You don't mean that it's an animal so small that it could—"

Kildare nodded, anticipating his words.

"I think you have the idea, doctor," be said briskly. "It was an animal as small as that. We saw it. It might have been a tiny lizard or a very small snake. I would say that Hazard has guessed correctly. It's my theory that the little beast poked its head up one of Gregory's nostrils and inflicted its poison that way."

The second officer shuddered openly.

"God!" he breathed. "That's a horrible thought."

"I agree with you," Kildare admitted.

The doctor turned to the three men.

"Give me a hand with the body, will you?" he asked. "I'll take it down to my cabin and make a complete examination at once. TWO HOURS later Kildare and Hazard, still attired in pajamas over which they had donned their dressing gowns were seated in the doctor's office. They had watched him as he cut away tissue from the nose and took tiny samples of blood. Now he held up one tissue that was marked with a single red dot, well back in the nasal passage.

"I think," he said, "we have it here. I'll make tests of the juice of the tissue."

It was nearly dawn when he looked up from the stiff body of a rat that he had experimented upon.

"I'm sure," he said, "that Gregory's death was caused by a venomous poison. It's a poison that instantly paralyzes the entire nervous system. Death, I should say, would come to a human being in five or ten seconds."

The two Americans returned to their state-rooms.

"That was a clever piece of work, figuring out where the poison was injected," Kildare said. "I think you and I are going to get along together famously—that is, if you care to see the job through and try to forget Mohra."

As he spoke, a knock sounded on the door. The room steward handed him a wireless message in a sealed envelope. Kildare tore it open and they read it together.

> HAVE NO KNOWLEDGE OF GIRL OF YOUR DE-
> SCRIPTION WORKING WITH W.F.
>   CHIEF INSPECTOR. SCOTLAND YARD.

"You see?" Hazard demanded triumphantly, "you've just let your imagination run away with you, Kildare—at least so far as the girl is concerned."

Kildare smiled rather mysteriously.

"Perhaps," he admitted. "But at least my imagination wasn't wrong in connection with that stooped man."

"What's your theory on that now?" Hazard asked.

"Just about the same as before," Kildare nodded. "As I see it, this stooped man, whom Gregory called Jimmy, came to place that poisonous beast in my room. When Gregory caught him in the corridor he had to change his plans quickly and made up the story about being an office boy in Scotland Yard. Gregory invited him in for a chat, and he decided he may as well leave the little beast there. He had probably received orders to get both Gregory and me, so it didn't make a great deal who got it first. My turn will be next, perhaps tonight."

IF VAL KILDARE was worried about Wu Fang marking him for death the following night, he didn't show it all day. But as evening drew near and he and Hazard finished dinner, the nerves of the newspaper man began to tighten.

"Confound it, Kildare," he said at length, "I wish this voyage were over. I'd give anything if we were in New York right now."

Kildare shrugged.

"We would probably be in as much danger there—if not more. At least, we have one thing to be thankful for. Wu Fang is hampered more on this ship than he would be in a great city. There are fewer people and a larger percentage of them to watch for strange happenings."

"I wonder," Hazard ventured, "how many of Wu Fang's agents are aboard?"

Kildare smiled.

"I haven't the faintest idea. But that reminds me. Have you seen anything of Mohra since you took her to her stateroom last night?"

"No," Hazard said a little bitterly.

Kildare's smile broadened.

"She hasn't even left her cabin, has she?"

"How did you know?" Hazard demanded, shooting a quick glance at him.

"Only that I saw you hanging around the corridor near her room today," Kildare chuckled. "I imagine she will be out before long, though."

And much to Hazard's joy, that proved to be true. Toward the middle of the evening, Kildare suggested a whiskey and soda. Hazard hesitated.

"I think," he said, "I'll take a turn around the deck if you don't mind."

Slipping on his raincoat, he walked outside. The rain had let up enough so that there was only a driving mist, but the wind continued to whip up the sea into a froth of billowing waves that rose higher than they had at any time during the journey.

A little more than an hour passed. Hazard had met only a few people on the decks. The storm was keeping most of them inside.

He was struggling along the rail of the open top deck, moving toward the stern, when suddenly his eyes focused on a slim, graceful figure just ahead. Instinctively, his step quickened.

No one but Mohra carried herself with that easy poise, that panther-like swing of perfect limbs and body, even when struggling against the pitch of the ship along the outer rail. Just before he reached her, she turned and he thought she made a move to enter the next door. But then she stopped with a gasp.

"Oh," she exclaimed, "you startled me, Mr. Hazard. It is you, isn't it? I thought perhaps it was—"

She stopped short.

"Mohra," he said, joining her at the rail, "That's your name, isn't it?"

"Yes."

He saw her smile in the darkness and he thought it the sweetest smile he had ever known.

"Look here, Mohra," he hurried on. "You shouldn't be out here alone. Don't you realize that something might happen again tonight as it did last night?"

She straightened.

"You are sorry to see me?" she demanded coldly.

"Of course not," Hazard blurted. "Confound it, Mohra, I've been watching for you all day. Oh, I know I haven't any excuse for talking this way, but don't you see? After last night, after everything that has happened, I've been wondering about you."

Jerry Hazard was aware of an uncontrollable feeling of joy rushing over him, for the dark mysterious girl had laid a soft hand on his arm.

"It was very kind of you to help me last night," she said. "It is nice of you to worry about me, but—"

Her soft voice broke off as a gust of wind came slashing across the deck. The girl's hand left his arm and they both were forced to cling to the rail for support as the ship gave a mighty list.

Then he saw her face in the darkness and it seemed to have suddenly changed. Just a moment before, those wide, dark eyes had seemed almost happy. Now they were narrowed and flashing angrily. Her voice was still low, but it had suddenly taken on a sharp note.

"You will please stop following and watching me, Mr. Hazard," she said. "I am quite capable of taking care of myself."

Hazard stared for a moment in astonishment.

"But Mohra," he pleaded, "I can't forget last night. You were in danger. If Kildare and I hadn't come when we did, heaven only knows what might have happened to you."

She moved a few inches away from him along the rail.

"I can take care of myself," she replied. "You will please me much more if you attend to your own affairs."

Suddenly, she turned and with a movement so quick that Hazard was taken completely by surprise, she broke into a run toward the forward part of the ship.

HAZARD WAS after her in an instant. Even in the darkness, he saw the wind whip her clothing tightly about her, impeding her movements. But that didn't seem to daunt her in the least, for without the slightest hesitation, she picked up the skirts of her frock and coat, raised them above her knees, and struck out in a wilder dash of speed than he had dreamed she was capable of.

He was aware, also, of a shadowy form slinking in the opposite direction on the inside of the deck. He didn't take time to watch it at the moment, but he remembered it afterward.

Hazard was running as fast as his legs would carry him. There was speed in those legs, for he had done well in track at school a few years before. But the girl was drawing away from him.

She made a swift turn around the forward cabins just as the ship's nose burrowed into the trough of a great wave.

The movement of the boat threw him off his feet; spray slapped him in the face. He jumped up, raced on.

But when he rounded the forward end a deck door was fast closing. He dashed through it, paused for a moment to glance at the corridors which branched off to the right and left. He darted first to one, then the other, looking down both. But they were empty. Mohra, borne on her fleet feet, had eluded him completely.

He paced the lower deck torn with emotion. He wanted to go to her, demand an explanation for her strange conduct. Didn't he have the right? Certainly! Hadn't he and Kildare saved her the night before? All his tangled thoughts gathered together in a foggy muddle that made no sense from any angle.

At length, he took off his slicker and made his way to the bar where he found Kildare sitting alone in the same place they had occupied the previous night. He looked up over an untouched, frosty glass.

"Oh, there you are," he greeted. "I've got news for you. We're changing cabins."

Hazard gave a short nod. "That's the most sensible thing I have heard yet," he said.

Kildare shrugged.

"Oh, I had no part in it," he explained. "You see, I've sailed on The Bergenland before and know the captain fairly well; he seems to think I'm a good sailor. There is a certain Mr. Kitchner, an American merchant, whom the rough sea has been treating badly. He put in a request to have his rooms changed to the center of the ship, about where mine is located. You see, he has been occupying a suite on the deck aft. The captain asked me if I would mind making the change, since he knew I could get along almost anywhere. Of course, I agreed. Hope you don't mind."

Hazard shook his head vacantly. "No. No, of course not." Then suddenly he frowned.

"Look here, Kildare," he said. "Wait a minute. Do I get you right? Kitchner has paid at least a hundred or a hundred and fifty dollars extra for superior accommodations on this voyage and he's willing to swap it for your cabin?"

Kildare smiled.

"If you could have seen him, you wouldn't have wondered. The poor fellow has been sea-sick ever since we left England. And you've got to admit that he's in a bad position in the aft end of the ship in rough weather like this. I think you'll like our new quarters—I moved our stuff in nearly an hour ago."

Suddenly Hazard straightened. His troubles with Mohra were forgotten.

"But look here, Kildare," he argued. "You've put this man Kitchner in a very difficult spot. Wu Fang's agents have orders to get you. You said this morning that probably it would be your turn tonight. And now you deliberately put Kitchner in your room."

"I was wondering if you would catch that angle of it," Kildare said. "As a matter of fact, Kitchner is in your room, not mine. That's centrally located also."

He lowered his voice.

"I've said nothing to anyone about the change. I simply ushered Kitchner into your cabin and took our luggage from my room into Kitchner's suite."

Then, in a still lower voice, "Even Kitchner doesn't know he has your room. I haven't told the captain about it and I don't intend to. The purser has Kitchner registered for two-seventy three."

CHAPTER 7
MARKED TO DIE

"I THINK that puts a different light on it then," Hazard said. "Beyond a doubt, Kitchner will be O.K. in my room."

The waiter brought a drink that Kildare had ordered for him; he sat for a long time, staring down at it. Finally Kildare spoke softly, with a touch of humor in his voice, "Well, how did the walk go?"

Hazard shrugged.

"O.K."

But Kildare was not to be fooled.

"Come on out with it, old man," he ordered. "If we're going to ride this thing through together, we can't be keeping secrets to ourselves. You saw Mohra, didn't you? What did she have to say? You look as though she had tried to throw you over the rail."

"If she had," Hazard answered savagely, "I wouldn't be feeling much worse. Damn it all, I might as well tell you."

He recounted what had occurred on the top deck. Kildare leaned forward with interest.

"By George!" he said. "That's strange, isn't it? You are sure you didn't say anything to offend her?"

"No," Hazard shook his head slowly. "I wouldn't say anything to offend her for the world."

"But this shadow that you think you saw along the inside of the deck. Did you get a good look at it?"

"No," Hazard said savagely. "I wish I had, now, but I was so anxious to catch up with Mohra—" He bit his lips. "Damn it, I'm mad about the girl."

"Yes," Kildare smiled, "you didn't have to tell me that. She's beautiful There's no doubt about that, and her mysterious actions make her all the more alluring. That's part of the game."

"Game?" echoed Hazard. "I tell you, Kildare, it isn't a game with her. It's something else. Something has hold of her. I don't know what it is. She was standing there, telling me how grateful she was for our help last night. Then suddenly, a change came over her as though she had become an entirely different woman."

Kildare patted him on the shoulder.

"Take it easy," he advised, "and don't put too much trust in her. That's all. Drink up and then let's take a look through our new suite of rooms."

Hazard gulped down a drink and they rose from behind the table, went below decks. Now and then, Kildare glanced behind.

"Expecting someone?" Hazard asked.

The ex-federal man nodded. "Always. But we're not being followed now. I am sure of that. Just for luck, though, let's drop into my old room for a few minutes. I still have the key."

They turned into the private hallway where tragedy had reigned less than twenty-four hours before, and Kildare unlocked cabin two-seventy-three. They stayed there for about half an hour talking.

"I think we're perfectly safe now," Val said at last "Let's go."

He switched off the light, closed the door and they made their way to the deck below. Hazard stared in awe at the sumptuous suite of rooms.

"Not bad, eh?" Kildare demanded.

"I'll say," Hazard nodded. "Living room with a davenport and a couple of comfortable chairs and a lounge and desk and—" He looked in at the bedroom. "Say, this is something. Two complete, double beds and they're on the level. You don't have to climb to an upper bunk. And a private bath."

"Here's another thing that I like about it," Kildare said, moving back to the living room. "We have two entrances. One door opens directly on the deck and the other into the corridor that we just came through. We may be able to use this outer door to good advantage before we reach New York."

Hazard dropped into one of the easy chairs while Kildare stretched out at full length on the davenport.

"It must be swell to be able to travel in this fashion," Kildare went on, "with nothing to do but enjoy yourself and no threat of death hanging over your head."

Hazard frowned. "I don't know. I think I would get stale at it before very long."

"Guess maybe I would too. What do you say we take a turn around the decks and then hit the hay? Those beds look mighty inviting."

They were reaching for their slickers when the lights went out. Blackness—thick and impenetrable, descended upon the cabin.

With a startled oath Hazard leaped to the corridor door and flung it open, "They're out all over the ship!" he exclaimed.

Kildare was already at his side.

"Good Lord! Something devilish is up. Come on! Let's go out on deck."

There was a click as Hazard shut the door; then they were groping their way across the room to the other door that opened onto the deck. Kildare unbolted it sprang out A gust of wind slapped him in the face and hurled spray into his toughened skin. Suddenly, he stopped short, clutched Hazard's arm as a signal for silence.

"Look!" he gasped. "Is that something moving?"

Hazard blinked. His eyes weren't quite accustomed to the darkness yet. They were out on the deck now.

"There," Kildare explained. "See it? About halfway up the deck."

"Oh, yes," Hazard said. "It looks like a small man moving along on all fours. There he goes up the outside stairs to the deck above."

Kildare started forward. "Come on," he ordered. "He's moving fast. We've got to keep him in sight!"

THEY WERE at the stairs now, climbing up cautiously. At the top, he froze for an instant then suddenly broke into a wild run.

A shadowy figure was rising from a crouched position beside a state-room window not fifty feet away.

"Good Lord!" Kildare breathed, "Unless I'm crazy, that's the window of your cabin." He raised his voice. "Stop! If you move, I'll shoot!"

For a moment the figure flattened itself against the whiteness of the cabin wall. Then suddenly it dropped and started for the rail. Kildare raised his gun. Spurts of flame darted from the muzzle and the booming of the automatic echoed hollowly in the storm-tossed night.

The shadowy form seemed to waver for a moment. Then it gave a terrific leap for the rail, slammed against it, standing erect, and pushed over the side.

Both Kildare and Hazard reached the spot at the same time. They leaned far over. The ship had plunged into a heavy wave just at the instant that the crouched form reached the edge; now that side was lifting as the great ocean greyhound listed to the other side.

"Where is he?" Hazard shouted. "Can you see him?"

"No," Kildare yelled back above the wind. "He's gone over the side or—"

Shouts sounded from the forward end of the ship. Men were running toward them, carrying flashlights.

"What's going on?" several chorused. "What's happened? "What's all the shooting about?"

Then the flashlight beams riveted on Kildare and Hazard in the darkness. A tall, broad-shouldered man, the captain, stepped forward.

"Oh, it's you, Kildare," he said. "Who turned off the lights on the ship? What were you shooting at?"

Kildare thought quickly.

"A prowler," he said finally. "I think I got him and that the pitch of the ship threw him overboard. Either that, or he climbed over the side and in some miraculous way reached a porthole below; I can't believe that, though. It is too impossible."

Instantly, a half-dozen flashlights were turned down at the sea. The captain barked a command.

"Give the signal for reverse at once," he bellowed.

That order was relayed along the deck from one mouth to another of the crew. As the ship slowed its motion and went into reverse, the lights came on again. Two powerful searchlights, one on either end of the great liner, bored down into the churning water.

For perhaps twenty minutes the search went on, but without success. At the end of that time the captain drew Kildare aside.

"What do you make of it?" he asked.

Kildare shook his head. "I don't know," he admitted. "It's just as I told you, captain. The lights went out; we rushed on deck and saw this figure which we followed up the steps. We saw it crouched under the window of this cabin."

The captain stared at the window. Kildare and Hazard did the same.

"It's wide open," the captain said.

They rushed over to the window and peered in. Then Hazard's blood froze in his veins with horror as he stared into his own dark stateroom. A low moaning sound was coming from the direction of the lower berth. Suddenly, the groaning rose to a wail and next to a blood-curdling screech of terror!

CHAPTER 8
THE LITTLE MONSTER

JERRY HAZARD was trying to force his head and shoulders through the open window, but the casing was too small. Kildare grabbed him and jerked him back.

"Not that way," he said. "We've got to get in through the door. Come on inside."

The door was locked. Kildare drew back, then slammed against it with all his might, but to no avail. Again he lunged forward; the captain and Hazard joined him and beneath the charge of their three bodies, the door gave with a crash.

"Look out!" Kildare yelled. "Get that thing! There it goes, out of the window."

Hazard started for the door again. But before he reached it, Kildare's gun barked twice. A small form that for an instant had perched on the window ledge shot out and down to the deck.

Darting to the window, he saw a tiny speck rolling across the deck. He called to a member of the crew.

"Quick! Kick that thing back with your foot. No, no, for the love of heaven, don't touch it with your hand! Kick it back against the cabin."

The man kicked viciously. Kildare watched it for a moment. From what he could see, the little beast was perhaps four or five inches long and was blown apart in the middle where one of his bullets had hit it.

"Keep your foot on it," he ordered the deck hand. "If it moves, crush its head. Don't take any chances with it."

The state-room that had once been Hazard's was now flooded with light as someone snapped on the switch. Kitchner was lying in the lower bunk, writhing and yelling in agony.

Those were stout men that looked down at Kitchner. There were the captain and his second officer; there were Hazard and Kildare. All of them had seen strange and ghastly sights during their travels throughout the world, but never had their eyes bulged nor their faces whitened at such a sight as was before them now.

Kitchner was writhing in a series of convulsions. His stomach was bare and there was a hole in the middle of it that gushed blood and body fluid. Moreover, there were teeth marks where tiny, saber-like teeth had torn away the flesh.

The suffering man was trying to speak. He was very much awake, horribly conscious in his terrific agony. Between the screams of pain, he managed to get out a few words.

"Horrible face at window. I—felt something—jump to bunk.

It got—under bed-clothing. Tried—to catch it. Everywhere—I touched it—it stung me. The pain—can't stand it. For God's—sake, do something. Hit—me over the head. Kill—me. Get me—out of this."

All this was interspersed by screeches and convulsions of pain.

The captain had sent for the ship doctor some minutes ago. Now the medical man came dashing into the room, his black case in hand.

"Good heavens!" he exclaimed. "Another one!"

Then he stopped short and stared at the horrible sight. Even he, a doctor who had undoubtedly seen the most ghastly sights of them all, turned pale.

"Listen," Kildare snapped. "There isn't anything that can be done for him, is there? Except dull the pain. Give him hypodermics quickly."

The doctor nodded. His hands were trembling as he fumbled in his bag for his hypodermic needle and a drug mixture to fill it. Then, as Kitchner continued to writhe and scream with the torture of a thousand demons probing him, the doctor inserted the needle and pushed the plunger home. He stepped away for a moment and they all watched earnestly and prayerfully.

But there was no change in the dying man's actions, no let-up of the excruciating agony. The doctor's face turned white and he bit his lip. He fumbled in his black bag again, filled the hypodermic needle with another liquid and jabbed that into the skin.

"Good Lord!" he groaned. "Drugs haven't any effect on him!"

The little group of men stood there, helpless. There was nothing to be done. Kitchner continued to shriek out his agony.

Kildare stood it as long as he could, then turned to the captain.

"The man can't live. I don't know what poison it is, but he's as good as dead now. Have I your permission to—"

He moved the gun in his hand with a significant gesture.

The captain hesitated. The doctor's eyes were glued on the agonized face of Kitchner.

"Wait," he said. "Just a second."

Then the man who was suffering the tortures of hell rose up in the bunk. He shook mightily with a terrific convulsion. Then suddenly, the life seemed to go out of him and he flopped back limply to the pillow. They bent over him while the doctor made a quick inspection.

"Don't touch that wound in his stomach or any of the blood," Kildare warned.

"Don't worry," the doctor said. "I won't." A moment later, he looked up and nodded. "Thank God he's dead," he breathed reverently.

THE MEN that crowded the little cabin stood there for some time, looking dumbly down at the figure that a moment before had been racked with terrific pain. No one could think of anything to say. There wasn't anything to say.

At length, the doctor took a long breath. He had been the last to speak and the first to break the silence.

"What killed him?" he asked of Kildare.

"If you will come outside," Kildare ventured, "I'll show you the little beast that did it."

"Beast?" gasped the doctor.

Kildare nodded.

"Yes. Kitchner told us about it before you came. Apparently, it gnawed itself into his stomach and then inserted its poison. I shot it just as it was going over the window ledge. I'll show you."

They walked out on deck and a blast of saltwater-soaked air struck them.

"Phew!" whistled the doctor. "This is a little better. I have never experienced such a time in all my medical career. Where is it?"

"Right here under the window," Kildare said.

They had reached the point where the deck hand was still standing with his heavy shoe on the tail of the little monster.

"It's dead?" Kildare asked.

"Oh yes, sir," the deck hand stammered.

Using his handkerchief to protect his fingers, Kildare reached down and picked the thing up by the tail.

"Good heavens!" the doctor gasped as he stared at it "I never saw such an animal before in my life."

"Nor I," Hazard agreed.

It was a strange creature. Except for its head, it resembled a small lizard of the armor-coated type. From the tip of its pointed nose to the end of its tail, it wasn't more than four inches long. Small, thick scales covered the body and tail and each scale ended in a barbed point that protruded out like a sticker.

The legs were short with long, sharp claws that curved wickedly like talons. But the head was the most ghastly member.

THE CASE OF THE SIX COFFINS

Also covered with barbed scales, it resembled that of a rat in shape and appearance. The mouth was open and there were saber-teeth on both upper and lower jaws, curving forward so that they could rip with amazing speed.

The captain shone his flashlight on it at close range.

"You see," Kildare said with a voice that was a little shaky, "the two longest teeth, both in the upper and lower jaws, are hollow inside like the fangs of a poisonous snake."

"Just a moment," the captain said suddenly. "This evening, I asked you to change rooms with Kitchner. What was he doing in that other cabin?"

The federal man glanced about at the crowd that was gathering and lowered his voice so that only the captain could hear.

"I felt certain that I was marked to die tonight," he explained. "Therefore, I didn't want to put Kitchner in my room."

"I see," nodded the captain. "So you put him in Hazard's cabin."

For a moment he continued to regard Kildare through narrowed eyes. Then he gave a short nod and turned to the doctor.

"You will take charge of this animal, doctor. Make whatever disposal of it that you wish. Kildare, I would like to see you and Hazard in my cabin, if you don't mind."

When the door of the captain's quarters was closed behind the trio, he turned to the two men.

"Something has been going on here," he said, "that you've been keeping from me and I think it's about time I know what it is."

Realizing there was no longer any point in trying to work

alone, Kildare described in detail everything that had happened since the beginning of the voyage.

When he had finished, the captain frowned.

"There isn't a Chinaman on board," he said. "I can't figure out where that yellow devil can be. Why didn't you tell me about this before?"

"Simply for this reason," Kildare answered. "Right now I'll guarantee that the thing uppermost in your mind is an immediate search of the entire ship. That will mean only that you will lose ten or fifteen, possibly twenty members of your crew, before the search is over—and I doubt very much if you will find Wu Fang."

"Do you mean to tell me," demanded the captain, "that a man can hide on this ship and we can't catch him?" There was a note of disgust in his voice.

"I mean," Kildare asserted, "that Wu Fang would kill every person aboard before he would be taken prisoner."

"That's possibly true," the captain admitted. "Nevertheless, he's not infallible."

Kildare shrugged. "Perhaps not," he admitted, "but he comes about as close to it as anyone I've ever heard of."

"But where could he hide?" the captain demanded again.

"For one thing," Kildare ventured, "you have a hold full of cargo. Why, there are any number of places where Wu Fang and his agents might find concealment. If we could narrow it down to some special quarter we might accomplish something, but to start out with no definite goal in view—" He shook his head—"No, it can't be done."

"But certainly you aren't going to permit him to reach New York," the captain protested, "and unload him and his devils without raising a hand to capture him."

"Oh, no," Kildare said. "Certainly not. I plan to radio the New York police and have police and Federal agents meet us in boats some fifty miles off shore; they would convoy The Bergenland into her dock, and keep the ship and passengers under constant guard. Every passenger and every member of the crew will have to give an accurate account of himself to the satisfaction of the police. Also we'll make a search of every piece of cargo as it's taken ashore. I think that when we reach New York, we will be able to corner Wu Fang!"

"Excellent!" nodded the captain, rising. "That will be the program then. Oh, just a moment. How about Kitchner being killed in Hazard's room?"

"Yes," Kildare nodded. "Here's the way I have figured it out. I took Kitchner, as I told you, to Hazard's room, expecting that he would be safe there. But one of Wu Fang's agents must have seen me moving the luggage and guessed that I myself was going to sleep there."

"There's another thing that perhaps you didn't notice," Hazard ventured. "Kitchner is about your build and looked quite a bit like you, Kildare."

Kildare eyed him quickly.

"By George!" he said. "I never thought of that."

"Well, you can see, captain, how the thing worked. I wouldn't have done this for the world to anyone. Of course, Kitchner got what was meant for me."

"I am sure there was nothing you could do to help it," the captain comforted. "You did the best you could to protect him. Good night, and don't worry about it. It's done and the main thing we've got to do now is to get Wu Fang."

"Right," barked Kildare. "Goodnight, sir."

THE TWO men were silent when they reached the suite. Without a word, they undressed. Hazard lighted a cigarette while Kildare puffed at his cigar and they dropped down in two easy chairs in the living room for a smoke before retiring.

Hazard was staring at the rug before him, staring hard and thoughtfully. Finally he roused himself.

"I don't know," he said, "whether what I'm going to say has any bearing on the case at all. It sounds rather ridiculous. I hope you won't think my imagination is getting the best of me."

Kildare turned slowly toward him.

"Nothing could be too fantastic in connection with Wu Fang," he assured him. "What is it?"

Hazard was occupying the chair nearest the inner door of the stateroom. He blinked his eyelids, which were growing heavy, and stifled a yawn.

"Ho hum, I'm getting sleepy. I'll just tell you this before I turn in. When I took my story up to the wireless operator—"

He felt his voice trailing away and snapped up to a full awakening again.

"Are you with me, Kildare," he asked, as he saw the other's eyes drooping. "I don't want to bore you with this if you're too sleepy."

"No, no," Kildare protested. "Of course not. I'm listening. Confound it; I haven't been so sleepy in weeks."

"It was just this," Hazard said.

"The wireless operator told me that we were in for bad weather because there are a half dozen stiffs on board and a lame man and a hunchback on the passenger list."

Kildare sat up with a start.

"What's that? What did you say about stiffs? You mean bodies in coffins?"

Hazard nodded vacantly. "Yes." His voice sounded far off now. "Six coffins on board. I understand—it is rather unusual—to have six. Didn't carry that—many often."

Then, farther off still, he heard Kildare answer—"Six coffins—that's it. That's where—"

Kildare's voice trailed away. Hazard was trying to force himself back to full consciousness. This sleepy feeling wasn't natural. He wasn't sleepy; he was drugged. They were both drugged.

He made a mighty effort to force himself back to full consciousness. He managed to get his eyes open. He saw Kildare drop back in the other chair. Then a soft, soothing blanket enveloped him and he closed his eyes and slept.

Jerry Hazard awoke with a dull ache in his head. The light of day was streaming in through the shutters. His mind was sluggish, as though it were in a fog. He couldn't get his bearings, couldn't remember where he was.

He straightened with an effort and stared about him. Oh, now he knew. They were in the suite of rooms that had been occupied by Kitchner. Kitchner? Kitchner was dead. Then where had they been since then?

He was sitting up in one of the easy chairs of the living room, and was dressed in his pajamas. There were the ashes of a completely burned cigarette that had fallen to the table beside him. The ship was still rocking heavily. And there, over in the other chair, was Kildare, all spread out and asleep.

Suddenly, a panic of fear seized Hazard. He remembered they were talking about the caskets when they fell asleep. He recalled thinking they had been drugged. But how could they have been drugged? They hadn't eaten anything. They hadn't— perhaps it was the cigar and cigarette that they had smoked.

A fearful apprehension gnawed at his vitals. He got up with an effort, bent over Kildare. Suddenly he gasped in horror at what he saw. He couldn't hear Kildare breathing. He couldn't see any movement of life. And there, at the lower edge of one nostril, was a tiny drop of blood.

Instantly, his mind flashed back to the murder of Gregory and the mystery beast that had inflicted a wound in the tender membrane of the nostril. In panic, he caught hold of Kildare's shoulders and shook him.

"Kildare! Kildare!" he said. "Look at me! It's Hazard. Are you all right?"

But Kildare didn't move.

Hazard's nerves were ready to snap. He whirled to the phone on the wall, snatched the receiver from its hook.

"The doctor!" he shouted. "Send the ship doctor at once!"

CHAPTER 9
SIX COFFINS

IT WASN'T until twenty-four hours later that Val Kildare opened his eyes. The ship doctor had been in constant attendance; was in fact at his bedside when his eyelids lifted heavily and he stared about in bewilderment. He looked first at the doctor and then at Hazard.

"What happened?" he asked weakly. "I feel as though I had been pulled through a saw-mill."

The doctor smiled down at him.

"You've been pulled right out of the jaws of death," he said.

Kildare closed his eyes and let his head drop back on the pillow. Hazard stepped forward anxiously, but the doctor stopped him.

"He'll be O.K." he said. "Weak, that's all."

Again Kildare looked up.

"Here," the doctor, continued, "I want to give you another injection of anti-poison serum and then I want you to rest for a little while. When you feel stronger, we'll talk the whole thing over. Perhaps you can help us figure out what happened."

It was later on in the day, when Kildare felt more like himself again, that they began discussing the affair.

"Remember," Hazard explained, "how sleepy we were getting when I told you about the coffins on board? We were drugged. I don't know just how, though. Perhaps it was in the tobacco we smoked."

Kildare thought for a moment, then shook his head.

89

"No," he said, "that couldn't have been it. The cigar I smoked was in my pocket all evening. No one could have gotten to it to dope it."

"The same goes for my cigarette I was smoking," Hazard admitted.

"Then the thing was worked in some other way," Kildare guessed. "Perhaps through the keyhole. That's an easy trick. A drugged gas that has no odor is forced from a small compression tank through a keyhole or under the door with a rubber hose."

Suddenly he straightened.

"Good Lord!" he exclaimed. "The half of that note! That's what they were after. They couldn't find it when I was dressed because I was carrying it around with me. Hazard, look in the inside pocket of the suit coat I was wearing. I carried the note there in a wallet."

Hazard went to the coat closet, shook his head after a fruitless search.

"There's no wallet here," he said.

"That's it," Kildare nodded with a shrug. "Well, Wu Fang has all of his note now. I've lost the only sample of his secret code I've ever had plus a chance to strike a bargain with him. And he has the full name of the inventor—I imagine that is why he wanted the note." Hazard's eyes widened in horror. "Good Lord!" he gasped.

"I see you realize what it means?" Kildare went on. "The minute Wu Fang lands, he's going after George Opporte. He's going to learn the secret of that gas so that he can kill masses of people at will."

He stopped, panting for breath; then gathered his strength and raised up on one elbow.

"Do you understand?" he demanded, his eyes flashing. "It means that no one is safe if he gets hold of that invention, no one in the world."

The doctor pushed him back on the pillow gently.

"Calm yourself, Kildare," he advised. "It's been a tough job to pull you through so far. You can't have a relapse now."

Kildare relaxed and nodded. For a few minutes he lay motionless. Then he turned quickly to the doctor.

"You say you had a tough job pulling me through. What was wrong with me? It wasn't just the drug. Hazard's all right and he was in the same room."

"No," the doctor said, "it wasn't that. It was something else."

"You don't mean—the little beast?"

The doctor nodded. "It bit you in the nostril, the same as in Gregory's case. Why you didn't die is more than I can understand."

"I think I have an explanation for that," Kildare ventured. "It takes a long time for the poison sacs of venomous reptiles to secrete a full charge of poison. Perhaps the poison fangs of these little monsters are of similar structure. This little beast that attacked me might have been the same one that killed Gregory, and he hadn't yet developed a full charge of poison."

HAZARD STAYED with Kildare constantly during the

day that followed. In the afternoon, Kildare was walking about the room. Toward evening, he began getting restless.

"Tonight," he announced, "we're going to start searching those coffins."

Hazard's eyes narrowed. "Are you strong enough?"

"I'll get along," Kildare answered. "After supper we'll wait a couple hours and then get moving."

When they had finished dinner, which was served in the living room of the suite, Kildare sat at the desk and began scribbling. At length he walked to the telephone, called the wireless room and dictated a message.

"HAVE ALL POSSIBLE POLICE BOATS AND COAST GUARD CUTTERS WITH MEN HEAVILY ARMED MEET BERGENLAND FIFTY MILES OFF SHORE. WU FANG AND AGENTS ON BOARD. CONVOY TO DOCKS. LET NO ONE LEAVE SHIP WITHOUT EX-PLANATION. GUARD HOME AND LABORATORY OF GEORGE OPPORTE WITH ALL POSSIBLE CARE. PLEASE DISREGARD ANY POSSIBLE CHANGE IN MY STATUS AS THIS IS VERY IMPORTANT.
KILDARE.

"Send one message to New York headquarters of the Federal Investigation Bureau," he said, "and a duplicate to New York police headquarters."

He hung up the receiver and sighed.

"If some cocky brat in the receiving room doesn't pigeonhole this because I've been fired from the Bureau, we'll be lucky," he said.

He rummaged in his baggage for a few minutes, then looked up with a puzzled expression.

"That puts a little different aspect on the situation. I had two good guns, but they're gone now. Well, we'll have to go through with it barehanded, if that's agreeable to you."

Hazard forced a grin. "It doesn't sound any too inviting," he admitted, "but if you say so, I guess that's the way it will be."

They entered the corridor, started down it—and didn't see the captain until it was too late to back up.

"Oh, you're up," the captain said, apparently surprised. "I was just coming down to see you. I was wondering if you don't think it's time the ship was searched."

Kildare hesitated for a moment. "As a matter of fact," he admitted, "we were just about to start on that little job ourselves. We're due to dock at noon tomorrow, aren't we?"

The captain nodded. "Two o'clock. Suppose that I get the crew armed and we'll start a search."

Kildare laid a restraining hand on his arm. "If we turn the crew loose you're apt to have a panic among the passengers. But worse than that, Wu Fang and his agents will learn what's going on, and as I said before, that means somebody is going to be killed."

"But what else have you in mind?" the captain demanded.

"Simply this," Kildare explained. "It isn't very often that you bring six corpses across the Atlantic, is it?"

The captain hesitated. "No," he said, "it isn't."

"Then, perhaps," Kildare went on, "you haven't thought that six coffins would be an excellent way for Wu Fang to come aboard with some of his more ghastly agents that wouldn't tally so well as regular passengers."

"By George!" the captain exploded. "That's a thought."

"My idea is this," Kildare went on. "Suppose Hazard and I go down and have a look at the six coffins. Perhaps, to make it legal, it might be well to have you along, captain, since you are commander of the ship."

"I'll go with you gladly."

"Then," Kildare finished, "if we don't find what we're after in the caskets, you can turn your crew loose and make a thorough search."

The captain agreed. "We'll go at once, then," he announced. HE LED the way down one flight of stairs and then another. They strode through the engine room and then down another series of steps into the hold of the huge ship.

The light here was very dim at best. Cargo was piled high. Great boxes and bales had been fumbled together by the rough voyage. The aisles that had been left between, when the cargo was loaded, were practically obliterated.

Kildare stopped short once. Something had moved from the edge of a bale at his right.

"What's that?" he exclaimed shortly.

"A rat, no doubt," the captain said. "Let's hope so, anyway."

They moved on. But the captain was the next to jump back as something scampered in front of him. He took a long breath of relief.

"I guess my nerves are on edge, too," he admitted. "I didn't know there were so many rats in the hold. I'll have them exterminated when we reach New York."

It seemed, as they moved on, that everything down there was alive. The ship wallowed in the trough of a wave and then a great packing box rocked toward them.

"Run!" gasped Kildare.

They dashed for safety as the great box fell just where they had been.

"Just a moment more," the captain said through clenched teeth, "if you can stick it out. The coffins, I remember, were placed back here somewhere, here they are."

The captain had just uttered those words when, with the nerve-shattering abruptness of a heavy explosion, the dim lights went out. At the same time, the captain called out and they heard him leap forward.

Instantly, Kildare's hand dove into his pocket and he struck his cigar lighter. The flickering gleam of the flame showed the captain white-faced and shaking a little. He was looking around behind him.

"Damn those rats!" he exclaimed.

Then, from somewhere at the side between two packing cases, a gust of wind blew as though a human being had blown his breath. The cigar lighter went out. Kildare leaped back. At the same time, Hazard felt something brush across his face.

"Get him!" Kildare yelled. "Someone grabbed my arm. My lighter—it's gone!"

Then another light blinked in the pitch blackness of the hold.

A small green snake leaped from the coffin,

fastened its fangs in the captain's neck.

"Here we are," the captain sang out in a voice that was none too steady. "I've got a flashlight. Let me go ahead. Kildare, you and Hazard keep right behind me."

Reaching down, he picked up some stout poles.

"Here are some leverage poles," he said, "that they use for

moving the cases. We'll each take one and if anything comes near again, don't be afraid to strike to kill."

As they pushed on, something brushed close to Hazard. He struck out with the heavy lever—but it merely swept through thin air.

"I'd give a lot for three good guns and three flashlights," he breathed as they reached the caskets.

The coffins were packed in rough boxes and spread out in even double rows along an open space in the hold. Hazard shivered as the captain began unscrewing the top of the nearest.

"This is going to be fun," he said. "I can see that."

The screws creaked as they turned; they were all working at the job now. There was no sign of anyone to molest them.

Creak! Creak! Creak! went the last of the screws. The cover of the first box was coming off. The casket lay inside, fitting its rough box snugly.

They were unlocking the catch on the coffin now. The captain's hand trembled as he raised the lid. Then he darted back with a cry of alarm.

Something leaped from the casket as the cover came up. It was a small green snake. It didn't spring out like a rattler with a third of its body still in the casket, but it leaped a distance twice its length and fastened its fangs into the captain's neck.

He let out a cry of pain and ghastly fear, wavered for a moment, then toppled over, with his head and shoulders in the casket.

The flashlight dropped to the floor, but remained lighted. Kildare and Hazard both dived for it, but Kildare got it first for he was nearer.

"Get them!" he yelled. "Get those snakes! There's more of them, coming out of the coffin. Never mind the captain. He's dead now."

Hazard was swinging the club with all his might as the snakes threshed up before them. Kildare was trying to beat them down too.

THE CASE OF THE SIX COFFINS

And while they labored frantically there was a creaking sound as of a lid lifting. Simultaneously the hold was suddenly lighted with a weird illumination.

Before Hazard could turn he felt a slight sting, like a pinprick in his back. Then the burning feeling was gone and he was growing numb. He saw Kildare stiffen, saw him struggle to hold onto the flashlight, but it dropped to the floor along with his club. Both of them were slowly growing powerless to move and still they were standing erect. Horror was frozen on their faces as they watched that coffin. Snakes were still slithering out of it. Snakes—and ghastly small beasts of every description.

Then their eyes became uncontrollably glued on something else. They saw that the lid of the next casket had opened and from it was stepping a figure, a tall figure with narrow shoulders and a wide forehead and pinched features.

He was dressed in a heavily-embroidered yellow robe of silk. His long-fingernailed hands were clasped together before him as he smiled at them in a benign manner. His eyes were green and as he widened them, they glowed iridescently as though they had tiny jade lights in them.

"Ah," he said very softly and his voice might have been that of a kindly old professor speaking to his students, "it is at last my pleasure to come face to face with you, Kildare, and with you, Hazard, the most worthy assistant. I need not command you to make no movement, for already the paralyzing darts with which my agents have pricked your backs have rendered you helpless."

He walked toward them with great dignity.

All feeling had left Hazard and Kildare. They were standing like helpless statues. Slowly, Wu Fang unclasped his hands and raised them before his glowing jade eyes. He pointed at the reptiles and beasts that were now up crawling over the body of the dead captain, and uttered some jargon in a strange language that the dreadful creatures seemed to understand. They crawled back, one by one, into the coffin. Very slowly Wu Fang shook his head back and forth in a strong negative.

"No, my friends," he said, "the death that is contained in the casket is not for you. It is too quick, too merciful. I have a better end for you."

He clapped his hands twice in muffled tones.

CHAPTER 10
THE FIGURE IN BLACK

HAZARD SENSED something moving behind him, but the paralyzing fluid from the tiny poisonous darts that had struck him in the back had taken command of him so completely that he couldn't even turn his head. Someone had slipped up behind him though; he was sure of that. Then, out of the tail of his eye, he glimpsed a figure behind Kildare. The man was almost completely naked like the one they had seen attacking Mohra; there was a stench in the air from the filth of his body.

Suddenly, both Kildare and Hazard were falling over backward, like statues of stone. Then their fall was checked as hands grabbed them.

Two half-naked figures picked up their feet. Then they were being carried back toward the engine room.

Wu Fang marched ahead of them with a slow, measured tread. He was ghastly in his deliberation. Each time he looked at them, he smiled. He smiled, Hazard thought, like a benign devil if there were such a thing. When he reached a certain spot at the back of the engine room, he climbed a stairway that led to a platform above the hold floor like a small stage. Apparently, it had been placed there for workmen to stand on while they were repairing pipes and packing the joints of the great steam trunk lines emerging from the engine room.

It was strange how that paralyzing poison had taken command of them. Their skin and muscles were numb, but somehow there was a sense of feeling still left in their eyeballs and with those alone they could feel the terrific heat reflected from those steam pipes.

Wu Fang's green eyes shone as he turned to them.

"It will be my pleasure," he announced, "to see that you two gentlemen are kept very warm indeed while I go on about my work."

He nodded to his half-naked agents.

"Tie them here," he ordered, "each with his back to a steam pipe and his arms tied around at the other side of the pipe."

They were carried up to the platform and stood up once more like statues with their backs to the steam pipes. They knew those

THE MYSTERIOUS WU FANG

pipes must be blistering hot if touched, but as yet no feeling had returned to them.

Their tongues felt thick. Neither one of them could utter a word. Their sole means of expression was in their eyes and there was plenty of hatred in them as they stared at the fiendish, smiling face of the Dragon Lord of Crime.

They couldn't feel their arms thrust behind them and tied around the hot steam pipes, but they knew it was being done. Only their sense of hearing remained clear to them, in addition to their sight.

Now Wu Fang commanded, "You will place a gag in the mouth of each."

His repulsive agents did their work swiftly. Then, at a word from their master, they leaped from the platform and scooted away among the packing cases like so many rats.

Wu Fang stood in front of Kildare and Hazard now, his long-nailed, yellow fingers clasped before him.

"You will remain there until death releases you," he said. "You will find, if you take my advice, that you will be more comfortable if you stand erect and don't touch the steam pipes with any part of your body."

His smile broadened.

"Ah, but already I know, gentlemen, you are saying to yourselves that the paralyzing drug will keep you from feeling the pain. That will only be for a few more minutes. In ten minutes, at least, the effect will wear off. Then you shall feel the burns which will be inflicted upon you if you lean against the pipes. I warn you, it will be a horrible pain, but a pain, nevertheless, that must be suffered by the enemies of Wu Fang. When you have regained your senses, what will you do? You will try to talk with each other. You will try to find some way of escaping. But there will be none. I can assure you of that. My agents do their work well. And so, while you stand there, gentlemen, blistering in the terrific heat, remember this: Wu Fang will not be captured by your dragnet police boats that you have ordered sent out. You are wondering how Wu Fang knows this?"

He chuckled in the tone of a kindly old man laughing over the antics of his grandchild.

"Wu Fang makes it his business to know everything. My agents and I will escape from the ship before we reach the fifty-mile limit outside of New York."

He chuckled again; his green eyes had never wavered from the two faces before him.

"I even know at the moment what you are thinking. You are thinking that the crew will stop me from leaving."

His eyes widened and that iridescent, jade-green light came into them, shining with hideous brilliance.

"The sea is growing calm," he said. "In a few hours, a little past midnight, the engine room will blow up. You are standing with your backs to the engine room, gentlemen. You know what will happen to you. But first, you will be heated thoroughly for the hell to which you will go when the explosion comes. Believe me, the officers and the crew of the ship will be very busy at the moment Wu Fang and his agents escape."

He bowed low.

"I will leave you now, gentlemen. And may your God have

103

mercy on your souls. There will be no more mercy given you in this world."

Majestically, he walked down the stairs from the little platform. The bulging eyes of Kildare and Hazard watched him as he threaded his way between the cases and boxes until he suddenly vanished from sight.

MINUTES PASSED. Suddenly, Hazard was aware of a tingling of his nerves. Wu Fang had spoken the truth. His senses were returning to normal. He was already aware of a hot, burning sting along his back, under his arms.

With an effort, he stood erect and moved away from that hot steam pipe around which his arms were bound. He bowed out his arms so that no part of his body touched that hot pipe. Even at that, the heat was almost unbearable. He felt the sweat oozing out all over his body.

The weird luminance in the hold had faded now and the ordinary lights had come on again as mysteriously as they had gone out.

Hazard heard Kildare mumbling, turned his head. Kildare was looking at him with an agonized expression and seemed to be chewing at the gag that was stuffed into his mouth. Hazard instantly began working at his own gag with his teeth and tongue. It had a vile and filthy odor, mingled with something slightly like oil. The taste and smell turned his stomach, but he kept on chewing. He saw Kildare spit out a piece of rag from under the tightly bound cloth and an instant later his mumbled words became distinguishable. "How are the bindings on your wrists, Hazard?"

Hazard tried to answer, but only a jargon of mumbling came. He chewed on and on, savagely, desperately.

The pipe seemed to be searing his entire back. Still, he could stand it. He couldn't do anything else but stand it. If his legs gave out and he leaned back he was doomed to terrific burns.

After several minutes of frantic gnawing he managed to separate a fair-sized piece of stinking, rotten cloth from the main part of the gag, and worked it out with his tongue.

"I think I can—talk now, Kildare," he said. "Can you understand me?"

Kildare nodded. "Yes. How are the bindings on your wrists?"

Hazard strained at them. While he worked, Kildare called a warning, "Don't let any part of your body touch the pipe. It's hot as blazes."

"Yes," Hazard agreed, "I've got a couple of good burns already."

After ten minutes of desperately cautious struggling at those bindings, he shook his head exhaustedly.

"It's no use, Kildare. I can't make it. How about you? Any luck?"

"None," Kildare moaned back. "Those devils certainly know their business. I guess we're about done."

"Do you think," Hazard mumbled, "that the engine room is really going to be blown up?"

"Positive of it," Kildare nodded. "If Wu Fang said so."

"How soon?"

"Hours probably," Kildare ventured. "My guess is that yellow devil will wait until two or three o'clock in the morning before he strikes. Everything will be fairly quiet on the ship by then."

"But look here," moaned Hazard. "Don't you suppose they will miss the captain and come looking for him?"

Kildare shook his head. "They would never think of looking for him in the hold. No one but us knows he came down here."

Hazard groaned. The steam pipes and the platform on which they stood were vibrating constantly with the steady rumble of the ship's engines.

"How about calling for help?" he suggested.

"No use. We can barely make each other hear what we're saying. I tried to yell a while ago, but I can't yell as loud as I can mumble. Try it and see."

Hazard took a long breath and let out what he expected to be a shrill cry for help; but the sound was muffled so that it was scarcely a sound at all and in straining to force it out, he pressed his arms unthinkingly against the steam pipes. His effort ended in a groan of pain.

Then they lapsed into silence, a silence that was broken only

He gasped one word under his breath—"Mohra!"

by the noise of the ship's engines. It was an ominous and ghastly silence, for with each rumble of those great engines, they knew they were being taken nearer to their destination. They were coming closer and closer to the horrible death that awaited them.

AN HOUR passed, then another and another. They dragged

on into an eternity of torture. There wasn't only the torture of the terrific heat; there was the mental torture. That was what Wu Fang had intended. He wasn't giving them a quick death that would be over soon, but the long-drawn out torture of waiting, waiting, in the terrific heat, not knowing what moment would be their last.

And all of that time they must stand erect. The only thing against which either of them could lean were the steam pipes around which their arms were bound, but that wouldn't mean relief. It would be added torture. Hazard had to grit his teeth several times to stay erect.

The ship was moving quietly now in a comparatively calm sea. That was something to be grateful for, anyway. If this had happened during the rougher weather, they would by now, in all probability, have been steamed to the tenderness of a pot roast.

Still another hour passed. It must be well past midnight. Any moment might be their last.

Beside all his suffering Hazard was dead for sleep. He felt himself slipping twice. The second time he forced himself to a full awakening he heard Kildare mumbling something.

He turned his head quickly and looked at him in sudden fear. Perhaps the man was out of his head. But no, he wasn't. He was perfectly sane and his eyes were narrowed.

"Look Hazard," he breathed, "See down there at the far end of the hold? No, over to the right. That's it. The light is very dim; you can just make it out. See what I mean? A crated speed cruiser."

A creaking sound came from the direction which Kildare indicated, a creaking sound as though nails were being pulled from their sockets.

"See what's happened?" he continued.

Hazard stared, wide-eyed. He made out the speed cruiser, saw figures moving about it. Again and again he heard the creak of nails being drawn. They were tearing the crate away from the boat.

"That," Kildare announced, "is Wu Fang's method of leaving The Bergenland."

"But how are they going to launch her?" Hazard asked.

"That speed cruiser was—the last thing to be put on board. Its right in front of the great side doors that open almost at water level. Wu Fang and his agents will put rollers under the boat, shove it over to the doors, open them—and then it won't be long for us. Unless I'm crazy, the engine room will be blown up just about the time the speed cruiser is launched.

Again Kildare and Hazard strained at the ropes that bound their wrists, but the ropes seemed to hold even tighter than before. At last they gave up and stood silent, watching the agents of Wu Fang work.

Suddenly, out of the tail of his eye, Hazard caught something else, something moving below the platform.

"Look, quick!" he hissed to Kildare, "what's that coming toward us?"

He heard Kildare's gasp of astonishment as he turned his head.

"Good Lord! It's coming up the stairs!"

CHAPTER 11
WU FANG ESCAPES

THE FIGURE flattened itself against the wall as it moved. Head, shoulders, and body, it was completely swathed in black. Like a token of death, it reached the top of the steps and crouched.

It was Hazard who cried out as loudly as the gag would permit, "Kildare—a knife!"

He had caught the gleam of a blade protruding from the black cape that covered the figure. There was no face visible.

Moving like a creeping shadow, the figure came on. It reached Hazard, and as it moved behind him he saw a hand outstretched in the dim light. It was a slim, white, clear-skinned hand with long, feminine fingernails. He gasped one word under his breath, "Mohra!"

Lips hidden by the heavy black veil cautioned, "Sssh!"

Then he felt the knife saw at the cords binding his wrists.

"If you have any regard for me," the girl said as she worked, "and for my safety, you will remain here a few minutes until I am out of sight. I have your promise?"

Then, at close range, Hazard glimpsed the lovely face of Mohra very dimly through the veil.

"Of course," he said quickly.

He heard Kildare's mumbled voice. "We promise. We will stay here until you are out of sight."

Hazard felt the ropes around his wrists loosen as the little dagger severed them. Then the girl moved on to Kildare, spoke again.

"It would be best if you slip away slowly," she said. "If you take my advice, you will not attack."

The veiled head moved significantly toward the speed cruiser that was now completely uncrated and ready to be moved out through the doors when they opened.

"You are unarmed," she went on. "You will only meet your death. Try to save as many of the crew and passengers as possible."

"But Mohra," gasped Hazard, "what does it mean? You've got to tell me. I've got to know. What are you to—"

The head beneath the veil shook negatively. "There is no time now. Do not think too harshly of me. Remember your promise."

Then she slipped away down the stairs and disappeared into the darkness of the hold the way she had come.

For a moment, the two men stood stunned. Their arms were released and their wrists were unbound.

"Take it easy," Kildare said. "They may be watching us. It's pretty dim up here."

He tore off his gag, and Hazard followed suit.

"What do you plan to do?" Hazard asked.

Kildare hesitated, then gave a quick nod.

"I think Mohra's judgment is best," he admitted. "It wouldn't do us any good to attack Wu Fang without weapons. We must reach the engine room and get everybody out before the explosion."

They began moving slowly off the platform down the steps.

"Can't we find the explosive?" Hazard suggested.

Kildare shook his head.

"There isn't time. It might be hidden in a thousand different places. Wu Fang might even have developed a time stoppage in the boilers so that they will blow up at a certain time. Our only hope is to save as many lives as possible and then we may have a chance to shoot Wu Fang from the decks."

They were in the hold now. They dodged around packing cases, as they ran for the engine room. Quickly they reached it and burst in.

"Run! Run for your lives!" Kildare shouted. "The ship is going to blow up any minute!"

The engine crew stared for a moment. Then there was a wild rush for the stairs with Kildare and Hazard leading the way. They raced up stairs after stairs, going higher and higher in the ship. Kildare was heading for the bridge, and reached it in a second's time.

He rushed into the control room.

"Quick!" he shouted. "I want the first officer. The captain is dead. Who is next in command?"

The second officer whom he had met before, dashed up.

"What's been happening?" he demanded.

As Kildare was explaining hurriedly, the first officer arrived.

"Wu Fang is leaving in the speed cruiser that was crated in the hold, the last thing you brought on board. Remember?"

The first officer nodded. "Yes," he snapped.

"It was a special job," Kildare went on, "built in England. He's going to shoot her out of the loading doors, and the explosion is going to come any minute. Get as many guns as you can. Hazard and I want one apiece, at least."

The first officer hesitated. "I've got only a few small arms," he said.

"Good Lord! Haven't you a one-pounder on board?"

"No. Come this way. I'll hand out the guns."

He dived into a cabin behind the bridge, opened a cabinet and began distributing a dozen-odd Colt automatics and ammunition.

Suddenly, he stopped short. The whole ship was trembling. From somewhere in the bowels of The Bergenland there came a rumbling sound that grew into a roar.

"THERE SHE goes," Hazard exclaimed. "Thank heaven we got everybody out of there before it was too late."

They burst out on deck. Kildare whirled to the second officer.

"Wireless the police in New York and tell them what has happened," he ordered. It was dark as pitch out there on the hurricane deck. "Tell them," Kildare raced on, "that—"

Blam! A sharp explosion close at hand cut off his words. Flame tore up and the second officer groaned.

"It's too late. There goes the wireless control room."

"Quick!" snapped Kildare. "Turn on the searchlights. Down on the water where the loading doors lead out of the hold."

He ran with the first officer toward a searchlight on the stern. It flashed on. For a moment, a piercing beam of yellow shot out over the ocean, then, slowly, maddeningly, it went out. Another petty officer came running up.

"The lights are out all over the ship," he shouted.

"Any flashlights?" Kildare demanded.

"I'll get some," he heard the second officer answer.

Then he was diving into the same cabin where he had secured the guns. He emerged a moment later, a very dim shadow in the darkness of the night. Then a light glowed in his hand and he was passing out flashlights.

"One thing more," Kildare snapped. "Better get the passengers in life boats. But first, I want to make a request. It's a little unusual under the circumstances, but it's our only chance of catching Wu Fang."

As he spoke, he leaned over the rail and shot the beam of his flashlight down alongside the ship. The great loading doors at the edge of the sea were gaping wide open.

"There she is!" Hazard yelled suddenly. "And is she making time!"

His light was trained out on the ocean and in its pale yellow glow, a speeding cruiser was visible. Kildare lifted his automatic. He pulled the trigger as fast as he could move his finger. Tiny spurts of flame darted from the muzzle into the blackness. Other shots rang out.

"Think we made any hits?" asked the first officer.

Kildare shook his head. "No," he snapped. "She's moving too fast. God, what I would give for a one-pounder!" He whirled. "Look here, as I said before, it's a little irregular, but you have a motor launch beside all the life boats. Hazard and I must take her and try to catch that cruiser. We're cut off from all possible help—wireless and engines gone. We'll meet the police boats as soon as we can."

The first officer hesitated a moment, then nodded.

"O.K. She's up forward. Climb in and we'll lower you away. We have life boats enough to take care of all the passengers and crew. The sea is calm and we ought to get by without any casualties if we're picked up soon enough."

"How far are we from land?" Kildare demanded.

"About a hundred miles."

A few minutes later, he and Hazard were in a launch down in the gentle swells of the calm ocean. A searchlight on the launch's prow flooded across the water, but it picked nothing out of the blackness.

Kildare looked over the side at the waves that the launch plowed up as it pushed through the water, and cursed.

"We're not making half the speed that Wu Fang was making," he groaned.

At dawn, there was no sign of any craft in any direction across the blue expanse of ocean. At last a line of smoke appeared on the horizon to the west, followed soon by the stacks of a ship.

Kildare, who was steering, turned the craft so it would cut across the bow of the steamer. Nearly a half hour later they were alongside, calling to the captain who leaned over the rail and telling him of the plight of The Bergenland. Then they plowed on.

Far off, they sighted a coast guard cutter heading toward them. There was a scramble on board when the boats met and after Hazard and Kildare told their story, wireless messages were sent to New York authorities. Also orders were broadcast to all other police patrol boats and cutters that had come in response to Kildare's radiogram.

The search of Wu Fang's fast cruiser went on up and down the coast until mid-afternoon, but without success. It was as though the boat and its crew had dropped from sight.

It was evening when the cutter which was carrying Kildare and Hazard steamed up the Hudson.

KILDARE TURNED to the commander. "You'll explain our hasty departure to the coast officials, won't you, captain?" he asked. "We've got to get in touch with a certain party at once. You can contact us any time you like through the New York Police or the Federal Investigation Bureau. I'm going to the latter place now."

A taxi whirled them to the bureau where Kildare was greeted heartily by the agent in charge.

"By George, Kildare," he said, "it's good to see you back. We heard something about your being discharged. What's all the fuss?" Kildare smiled.

"Simply a matter of reports," he said. "I'm positive that Wu Fang has agents in the bureau in Washington."

His friend nodded slowly. "I see." An ugly gleam came in his eyes. "But you're sticking it out, aren't you?"

Kildare gave a short nod. "You're right, I am."

"That's the stuff," the other commended. "And I'll guarantee that this office will ride with you and give you all the cooperation we can."

"Thanks," said Kildare. "I wanted to hear you say that. Right now, I'm going over to see George Opporte. He's the inventor of a deadly gas. I want to get all the dope on it and of course I want to be sure that I can keep my badge. It's apt to come in handy."

The other smiled.

"If anyone asks me about your badge," he said, "I'll tell them it's been lost. Go to it and good luck, old man."

Outside the bureau office, Hazard hesitated.

"Kildare," he said, "I'm sorry, but I ought to report to my syndicate office. Suppose I do that and join you at Opporte's place. What's his address?"

Kildare nodded. "O.K. I'll be looking for you."

He gave Hazard an uptown address, men each man climbed into a separate taxi and started for his destination.

Hazard went straight to his office. The chief frowned as he entered, then beamed.

"You, Hazard! Of all people! I'm glad to see you. Rotten luck on news, too. Just the usual run of European and South American troubles. Mighty nice story you sent in about the Chessfield affair, but that burst out in print five days ago. We've been following it up with a lot of guess work, but everyone's clamoring for more dope."

Hazard bit his lip.

"I haven't got any more dope on it," he said, "but you can take my word that some things in connection with that are going to break wide open and it will be the biggest yarn you've ever printed."

"Good," nodded his grizzled chief. Then he uttered one word which means everything in the newspaper racket. "When?"

"Just as soon as we can break it wide open," Hazard nodded. "I hope it won't be long. And you can jot this down. 'Bergenland blown up a hundred miles off coast. Hint at sabotage. Wireless apparatus destroyed!' No, wait a minute. Forget that last."

His chief looked at him sharply. "Say, what is this, anyway? Are you holding out on me?"

"I'm holding out on nothing that isn't of the greatest importance," Hazard snapped back. "Of the greatest importance, chief, to my life and the life of a friend of mine. I'm bound by a promise not to say too much until the thing breaks wide open."

"Oh, yeah?"

"Yeah," nodded Hazard.

His chief's eyes narrowed. "And when it does break," he demanded, "do we get the scoop on the whole story?"

"Yes," Hazard cracked, "and believe me, it will be a story that will make your hair curl. You can put this in your story of The Bergenland explosion. 'Calm sea. Think that all passengers have been saved. The captain—'" He paused for a moment and then went on. " 'The captain fought valiantly to stop the explosion, but was killed. *S. S. Stuyvesant* is racing to the rescue.' "

Again the chief looked up and eyed him coldly.

"You were on The Bergenland, weren't you?"

"Yes."

"Well then, how about those mysterious killings on board and the order to police and coast guards to convoy the liner in?"

"O.K.," Hazard nodded quickly. "Put all that in too, if you like. Any part of it will make a good story. String it along until I get more dope for you, but—"

He snapped the paper on which the chief had been writing with his index finger.

"Remember this," he went on. "If you want a scoop on the biggest and best story that has hit the newspapers in years—don't mention any names except the names of the victims. Build it up as a horror mystery. Gregory, a Scotland Yard man; Kitchner—I think he was a merchant; and of course, the captain whose death I have explained. Sorry, but I've got to run now."

"O.K.," the chief drawled, "but remember, we're counting on a scoop or your neck will be in a noose, Hazard."

Jerry Hazard grinned.

"Listen, chief," he said. "Either I'll bring in a scoop on the whole thing when it breaks, or they'll bring me back—stiff."

CHAPTER 12
A SUMMONS IN THE NIGHT

A DRIZZLING rain was falling upon the darkened city when Hazard left the syndicate office. Street lights blinked uncannily.

A small figure separated itself from the gloom of a doorway that had given it shelter and ran up to the reporter. It was a boy, who carried a few papers under his arm. He was perhaps fifteen years old, maybe only twelve. No one had ever known his age for certain. He had a strong, lithe body and a face that everybody remembered for its perpetual grin. Now he burst out in a wild greeting for his idol.

"Holy Gee! It's swell to see you back, Jerry. I didn't know if you would ever come back again. I've been asking the gang around the office about you. Gee, that post card you sent me from Paris was swell."

Jerry stopped stock still in the drizzling rain. A grin of pleasure spread over his face as he looked at the little fellow.

"Well, bust my buttons, if it isn't Cappy!" he said. "How are you, kid? So you got my card from Paris?"

"You bet I did," Cappy said, "and I showed it to all the other kids, too. Boy, you should have seen their eyes pop out of their heads! Are you going to stay now for a while, huh? Gee, listen. Remember what you told me to do when you left, Jerry?"

Hazard looked undecided for a moment. He was getting anxious to be off.

"I mean about the Boy Scouts," Cappy hurried on. "You told me I would learn a lot if I joined up with the Boy Scouts. Well, I did. I joined up right after you left. Gee, its swell and the stuff I learned!—"

Hazard patted the boy's shoulders affectionately.

"That's swell, Cappy, but I've got to go. I've an important assignment to cover. See you later."

Cappy grabbed his arm and clung to him for a moment.

"Oh, listen, Jerry," he pleaded. "You always promised you would take me on one of these assignments. I'm going to be a reporter like you some day. No fooling, I am. How about taking me with you?"

Hazard shook his head. "Can't be done," he said. "Not tonight. Might be danger in it."

"Aw," Cappy coaxed. "That would be swell."

Hazard shook his head more firmly. "Nope, not tonight. Some other time, Cappy. So long. See you later."

As he finished, he hailed a cab that careened to the curb. He climbed in, slammed the door, gave the driver the uptown address.

A half hour later, the taxi pulled up before a brownstone three-story residence. Hazard leaped out. He saw a police officer half hidden in the shadow of the basement entrance under the high steps. On the street he saw another figure move out of the shadow of the fourth house beyond.

Suddenly, he jumped. From behind him there sounded a shrill cry of "Wux-tra! Wuxtra! All about the big murder! Paper, mister?" There, running up before him, was Cappy. Hazard glared for an instant, then he had to laugh.

"Hey, what goes on here?" he demanded, not unkindly. "I told you that you couldn't come along tonight."

The boy's voice was low, almost a whisper.

"I know, Jerry," he said seriously, "but listen. You said this was dangerous and if there's any danger you're walking into, I want to be there with you, so I hopped on the tail of the cab and came along. Please, Jerry, can I come in with you?"

Hazard gave a determined shake of his head.

"For the thousandth time, no!" he said vehemently. "Be a good guy and go on back to your stand, will you?"

"Aw, gee," Cappy said.

Jerry Hazard turned abruptly and ran up the steps. A third officer stepped out of the gloom of the doorway above.

"I'm Jerry Hazard," he said softly. "Kildare's inside, isn't he?"

The cop at the door nodded and stepped out of his way.

"He left word for you to go in. Go ahead."

As Hazard entered, he heard Kildare's booming voice. "That you, Hazard? Come on in. I want you to meet one of the greatest inventors of the times."

GEORGE OPPORTE was a little fellow, short in stature and slim. He looked at Hazard through a pair of horn-rimmed spectacles. When he acknowledged the greeting, his lips barely moved as he spoke.

They were in a front room which seemed to be part living room and part office. Back of it, a door stood open. Through that, the elaborate gadgets that make up a laboratory were visible.

"Opporte has just been telling me," Kildare said, "about his invention. Would you mind repeating so Hazard will know?"

"I shall be glad to," Opporte said. "That is, if he's not a newspaper man."

"He is a newspaper man," Kildare explained, "but he's O.K. He has promised not to divulge any secrets unless we both agree that it is the proper time. He is helping me in the investigation I mentioned."

Opporte nodded, turned to Hazard.

"I hope you won't think I'm a fiend when I describe this gas to you. You see I am a chemical inventor and developed this gas to be used in case of war. It's so destructive that whatever country could obtain exclusive right to it could conquer the world. You agree with me, don't you, Mr. Kildare?"

"Absolutely," Kildare nodded. "I saw the result of it at Chessfield."

Opporte shifted nervously.

"It isn't commonly known that my gas was the cause of those deaths, is it?"

Kildare shook his head.

"No, and I don't believe it will get out—at least until the whole thing is cleared up. But go on, please, Mr. Opporte."

"Well," Opporte continued, "it is a colorless, syrupy liquid, and is harmless as long as it is kept away from the air. The instant that air touches it, it turns into a heavy, odorless, colorless gas that stays close to the ground and spreads over an amazing area. It has no effect on the lungs of an animal or human being. In fact, a person may be doomed to death by it and not feel it at all. He goes right on breathing normally and continues about his duties. Then, gradually, poison spreads all through his system—but it isn't a gas poison. It is the poison from his body which isn't allowed to leave the skin pores." He straightened.

"In other words," he finished, "this gas acts upon the perspiration fluid of the pores. It hardens this fluid almost like tiny wedges of granite and in that way stops up all the pores. You have heard of animals and even people who have been completely covered with paint and died. The paint stopped the pores in the same way this gas does."

Jerry Hazard's face was a little white.

"Good Lord!" he gasped. "Why, an airplane load of that dumped over New York would kill every inhabitant."

Opporte nodded solemnly.

"That's right," he agreed. "Rather ghastly, isn't it? To be frank with you, I have been scared to death ever since I invented this stuff and learned its characteristics. When a bottle was stolen from my laboratory, I—well, I didn't know what to do. That was when I met Mr. Kildare. But—"

He settled back in his chair, drawing a long breath.

"I'm glad to say," he continued, "that I think the danger is—"

The jangling of the telephone bell on his desk stopped him short. He bowed to his two guests.

"You will pardon me, please, while I answer."

Kildare leaped up. "Wait a minute," he said, holding Opporte back. "Let me answer."

The telephone bell continued to ring while Kildare took out his handkerchief, inspected the mouthpiece, wiped it off carefully, and then wiped off the receiver.

"Hello," he boomed.

Hazard saw him hesitate, scowl as though he were trying to recall something.

"Yes, he's here. Who is this speaking?... Just a moment."

He turned to Opporte. "Do you know anyone by the name of Bridges, Charlie Bridges?"

Opporte smiled.

"Of course. He's one of my best friends. Here, I'll answer it." He took the receiver. "Hello, Charlie. Yes, this is George.... Oh, that was a friend.... What?... You're not kidding me, are you?... No fooling? Well, that sure is one on you.... Sure, I'll be right down. O.K.... I think I have enough to get you out."

He hung up the phone and turned around, laughing.

"That's a good one," he chuckled, "Charlie Bridges, this friend of mine, they've got him down at the precinct station. Said they hauled him in for going forty miles an hour past a red light and they think because he had a glass of beer that he's drunk. The poor fellow sounds as though he's scared stiff. If you gentlemen will pardon me for a few minutes, I'll go down and bail him out."

"Wait a minute," Kildare said. "Are you sure that it was your friend's voice?"

Opporte looked at him in amazement.

"Of course. I've known Charlie Bridges for years. Come now, this is a little too serious, isn't it?"

Kildare shook his head.

"If you had been through what we have in the last few days, Opporte, you wouldn't laugh at taking precautions. If you insist on going, well go with you."

"BUT I say," the inventor argued. "I'm no baby. As a matter of fact, I'm getting fed up with this constant guard."

"A man who has at his command the destruction that you have, Opporte," Kildare reminded him, "should not be allowed to go around without a guard—at least until we get Fu Wang out of the way. I won't hear of your going out of this house unless someone goes with you. That's final."

Opporte looked thoughtful for a moment, then be smiled.

"Perhaps you are right at that," he said. "But if I take you two gentlemen with me, there won't be anyone left in my house. Wouldn't it be more to the point if I took one of the police officers stationed out in front? You see, he knows who I am and might intercede at headquarters for my friend."

Kildare thought that over for a moment then gave a short nod.

"O.K. I think that will be all right."

George Opporte laughed lightly as he walked to the hall. They followed him that far, saw him take his hat off the hook and don his raincoat. Then he went out into the night.

Kildare and Hazard went back into the living room slowly. Hazard sat down, but Kildare lighted one of his long cigars and paced the floor. From time to time, he glanced at the phone and each time he shook his head.

"Confound it Hazard," he burst out at length, "I don't like it at all. Why in the devil would his friend have to get in a jam just at this time. I wonder if that crazy fool did take one of the cops along or if he decided to go alone."

"If you want to know what I think," Hazard cracked, "he strikes me as a pigheaded bird. Let's have a look. We can find out in short order by asking one of the cops at the front door. There were two of them there when I came in."

Without stopping for hats or coats, they strode to the front door and threw it open. The black drizzly night met them. A street light across the pavement glowed dimly. But there was no burly figure standing in front of the house. A small form darted from wider the great stone stairs. It was Cappy, running to them with his papers under his arm.

"See, Jerry," he breathed, "something funny happened."

Kildare looked at the boy and shot a glance at Hazard.

"Who is this?" he demanded.

"A friend of mine," Hazard explained. "A newsboy. He's OK, Kildare. He followed me here on the back of my cab. What happened, Cappy? Where are all the cops?"

"Well, gee," Cappy said in a half whisper. "I was walking up and down, making believe I was selling papers. Then about five minutes ago, somebody screamed for help down the block. It sounded like a woman. She sure sounded as if she was getting murdered, too. Gee, I never heard anybody yell like that in my life. It was awful."

"Yes, yes," Kildare snapped, "and then what?"

"Well then, sir," the boy raced on, "the two cops at the door started running up the street and the third cop that was down the block, he came running too. Gee, and they all got their guns out. I was going to run, too. Then I thought maybe I had better stay here. Then a man came out of the house and he looked around and saw me. He asked me where the cops were. I told him they had all beat it down the street when somebody had yelled for help. He said he guessed he wouldn't wait and he started on."

"Alone?" demanded Hazard, knowing the answer before he asked it.

"Yes, sir."

"Good Lord!" groaned Kildare. "It's a trap. The whole thing was a plant. That scream was to get the cops away from the front of the house and that telephone call—that wasn't Opporte's friend or if it was, he was calling under stress. Probably some of Wu Fang's gang were threatening to kill him if he didn't say what they told him to. Remember Opporte said he sounded as though he were scared stiff? Unless I'm crazy, Wu Fang's got George Opporte right now."

CHAPTER 13
MURDER TAXI

KILDARE WHIRLED to Cappy. "Which way did the short man go?" he asked. "Did you watch him?"

"Yes, sir," Cappy said. "He went down this way."

Hazard nodded savagely.

"He went in the opposite direction from that taken by the cops then."

"Yes, sir," the boy admitted. "The cops went west and the man went east."

"Did you see him turn the corner?"

"Yes, sir," the boy nodded. "He turned left."

"That's right," Hazard nodded. "That's the direction of the precinct station."

"Come on, Hazard," Kildare ordered, "and have your gun ready for action. We're in for plenty of trouble if we're too late."

Kildare was running down the cross-town street in the direction taken by Opporte. Hazard was a pace or so behind him and Cappy was keeping up with him in good shape. Hazard turned to him as he raced on.

"There's going to be trouble, kid," he snapped. "You'd better stay out of this."

"Maybe I can help," Cappy ventured and kept on going.

They had run perhaps half the distance between Opporte's house and the corner of the block when a shrill police whistle sounded behind them—to the west. Kildare slowed for an instant and looked back. The vibrant whistle was eerie in the gloom of the street.

The drizzling rain had increased in volume. The sidewalks were slippery and glistening in what light was shed by the few lamps.

"What's that mean?" Hazard demanded.

Kildare didn't answer directly. He stared again at Cappy.

"Are you sure the short man came this way?" he asked.

"Yes, sir," Cappy nodded. "I saw him. He turned north at the corner. He can't be more than a block ahead of us."

A taxi whirled up the street Kildare shouted, tried to hail it, but the car passed on.

He struck off again in another wild burst of speed for the corner. As they swung around and up the avenue, they found the street quite deserted.

Ahead, were the lights of a car pulled up at the curb. They couldn't see very plainly, but something was going on. They heard a low cry.

Then, as they dashed ahead with renewed speed, a figure that had been hidden in a dark doorway lunged out into their path. It was a man. He came staggering on like one who was very intoxicated.

"Look out!" Kildare barked—and ducked.

The staggering figure raised its right arm. They couldn't see the face or anything about the man very clearly, but against the light of a dimly glowing street lamp farther down along the curb, they made out that up-raised arm.

It was coming down, straight for Kildare's head. But he dived close and let drive with his elbow in the man's stomach.

Things were happening swiftly. Something white flew past Hazard's face. His first thought was that it was a white bird. Then he saw the object flash under the downward blow that was being struck at Kildare's head. There was a crash as of a heavy instrument against a mass of crumpled paper.

At the same time, a small boy dashed past Hazard and charged at the stranger, merging with the shadow of his legs. As the man fell he cursed in some foreign jargon.

Kildare was fighting his way up through that mass of white that had saved him from being struck. His hand grasped the right arm of the felling stranger. He wrenched something out of it—a stout club.

Grimly he brought the club down with all his might on the other's skull. There was a loud, thwacking sound as the small, blunt instrument connected. Then the attacker's body went limp, dropped to the sidewalk.

Hazard pulled Cappy away from the legs of the stranger.

"That was fast work, kid," he commented. "I didn't know—" a muffled cry down the street cut him off. Then there was a grinding of gears, the roar of a motor, and the car charged toward them.

"Jump!" yelled Kildare. "They're trying to run us down."

At that same instant, the car leaped the curb. It was a taxi, identical with hundreds of others; the headlights were not so bright as to blind them to that fact.

Kildare dived for a building. Hazard started to follow, then saw Cappy slip and fall directly in the path of the murder car. He paused long enough to grab the back of the boy's coat and haul him across the sidewalk.

The car was within ten feet of him and gaining surprising speed. He leaped just in time and landed in a doorway. Kildare slammed him back into a narrow passage.

Ping! Something came hurling through the air, jabbed into the casing beside the entrance. The light, glistened on it, revealed it was a dagger—a nasty, thin-bladed instrument, with a short handle.

Then the taxi was flashing past. Someone was crouched on the running board. As the car whizzed by the man who had attacked them, the one on the running board, reached down, grasped the body and dragged it aboard. The taxi swerved, swung off the sidewalk and back to the street.

KILDARE WHIPPED out his automatic, cursed as he tried to take aim in the darkness. Two yellow flames spurted from the muzzle of his gun in quick succession.

"Missed him, I'm afraid," he choked.

His hand closed over the handle of the dagger and he jerked it from the wooden door casing.

Cappy was picking himself up from the spot where Hazard had tossed him.

"Are you all right, Cappy?" Hazard shouted.

"Sure, Jerry," the youngster flung back. "Did they get away?"

"For the time being," Kildare snapped and ran to the curb, yelling, "Taxi! Taxi!" at the top of his voice.

A cab came leisurely around the north corner. Kildare waved his arms frantically.

The cab speeded up a little and then stopped at the curb. Kildare flung open the door, pushed the boy in, then Hazard, and leaped to the running board.

"Keep going as fast as you can," he ordered. "I'll take care of any speeding charges. See that tail light? Follow it."

The driver nodded and the cab jerked into motion.

Kildare stood out on the running board with the rain pelting his face. Hazard and Cappy were leaning forward, staring out through the windshield, following the red light of the fleeing cab.

Suddenly the light went out. Kildare cracked a hoarse command to the driver.

"Keep up with cab," he ordered. "If you ever drove like the devil in your life, do it now."

The motor roared and the taxi shot ahead in second gear. They passed one street and then another. Kildare was leaning far forward, his eyelids narrowed to protect his eyes from that cutting slashing rain.

"Next block," he yelled suddenly. "Turn left. That cab switched off its lights so we wouldn't be able to follow it, but I caught it in the street light. Take the turn as fast as you can."

Hazard could see the other cab make the turn. He saw it skid dangerously and knew from that that the driver was pushing it at top speed.

Except for a few other passing taxis, the streets were deserted. It was a nasty night to be out.

There was a squeal of brakes as their driver applied the foot pedal. The cab listed and the tires squealed as he spun the wheel for the turn. They rounded the corner with the cab leaning far over. Then they were streaking down that cross-town street, heading east.

"Look!" Kildare yelled. "They've got their lights on now. They're probably afraid the cops will stop them if they run without lights very long. Keep on their tail, driver. We've got to catch them."

The driver gave a short nod. "I'll do my best," he hurled back.

They whirled on for three more blocks. Now and then a pedestrian stopped to watch them tear along the street at breakneck speed.

At last Kildare opened the door and climbed in out of the rain. For a moment he glanced at the youngster crouched against the front glass of the tonneau.

"Son," he said, "you're as bright as they make them. What's your name? Cappy?"

"Yes sir," the boy answered.

"Well, Cappy, let me say this while I've got time. You're a brave boy. That was a clever stunt to throw your bundle of newspapers so that they came between my head and the club that devil was bringing down on me."

"And you should have seen the flying tackle he made at that fellow," Hazard cut in. "You're there with bells on, Cappy."

Cappy grinned, but he didn't take his eyes off the car ahead. As they passed an avenue corner, he turned his head.

"Gee, look! The cops!"

Both men turned instantly.

"Good," Kildare nodded. "That ought to help."

As he spoke a shrill blast of a police whistle split the rain soaked air. A low police roadster had speeded out of the avenue and was trailing them.

A few moments later it pulled up alongside. Kildare was fighting with the window; as he did so he heard the cab driver shout—

"The man inside said he would be responsible!"

Then the window came down reluctantly.

"I'm Kildare, Federal investigator," he yelled, and at the same time flashed the badge inside his coat. Get that car up ahead. Yes, the one with the tail light. Important as the devil."

"Right," the police officer called back.

Like a flash the police roadster was pulling ahead, tearing down the street. They heard the sound of its siren piercing the night air.

"It won't be long now," Kildare snapped. "I think for once we have outwitted Wu Fang."

They raced on for several more blocks, then saw the police roadster drawing up beside the other speeding cab. Kildare leaned over to the driver.

"The police car has got him blocked," he said. "Park behind as close as you can. And then you'd better duck. There may be some shooting."

"Yes—yes sir," the driver stammered.

There was a squeal of tires on the wet pavement as their cab swung to the curb and stopped. Kildare was out instantly, gun in hand. The rear door of the first cab was open. He charged it. Then suddenly stopped and stared. Not believing what he saw in the darkness he reached in and switched on the dome light.

"Is this the guilty one?" the officer demanded, indicating the driver.

Kildare shook his head. "No," he said. "Are you sure no one escaped?"

Both cops nodded.

"There was nobody in this cab when we pulled up beside it but the driver."

CHAPTER 14
THE BLACK ROOM

HAZARD FELT a limp, vacant feeling come over him as he stared at that empty interior. "But listen," he shouted, "somebody was abducted in this cab. We saw—"

Kildare cut him off savagely.

"Don't be crazy, Hazard. We've been tricked. We had the cab in sight until it turned east; the lights were off, the next time we saw it, they were on. Remember I remarked about it?"

"Yes," Hazard said blankly, "but that was only a few seconds."

"It was enough," Kildare cracked, "for the cab to duck into an alley and for this one to take its place."

The two radio cops were waiting.

"What do you want us to do?" one asked. "Shall we hold the driver?"

Kildare nodded. "Take him down and lock him up for the night." Then, in a low voice—"I don't think we can do anything outside of a charge of speeding. Try and send him up for thirty days on that. It will keep him out of service, at least."

"O.K.," the cop agreed.

Hazard groaned as the first cab and the police car moved on.

"What are we going to do?" he demanded. "Good Lord, Wu Fang has got Opporte."

"Yes," Kildare nodded. "And he'll torture the poor fellow until he is either dead or reveals the secret formula of this gas." Suddenly he turned toward the cab.

"Come on. Let's get in. I've got a hunch."

He pushed Cappy and Hazard before him, then climbed in himself and slammed the door.

"Turn over on First Avenue and drive like the devil," he ordered.

As the car lurched forward, Hazard stared.

"Why down First Avenue?" he asked.

"It's the only thing I can think of," Kildare said. "First Avenue will lead us straight into Chinatown. I think Opporte's cab is being carried in that direction."

As they tore along with the rain pelting down on the roof, he took two objects from his coat pocket. The first was the dagger that had been thrown at them from the murder taxi. It was a strange little instrument with a small, curved handle and a blade that curved back and then out again up to the point.

Clutching the handle in his big fist, he pulled his sleeve down over his hand.

"Ever see anything like that?" he asked Hazard.

Hazard hesitated, a little puzzled.

"No, I can't say that I have. Yet there's something familiar about it."

Kildare traced the curve of the blade with the finger of his other hand.

"It's quite distinctive, isn't it?" he went on. "I've seen daggers almost like this in curio shops and museums, but the only place where it seems to be native is in upper Malay. There's a small Italian settlement there. I saw a dagger used at that place identical with this one. I also saw a blade like it very recently."

Hazard's eyes widened. "You don't mean that—"

Kildare nodded.

"Didn't you see Mohra's dagger very clearly?"

Hazard stammered an answer. He couldn't seem to find words.

For now that Kildare had mentioned it, he remembered there had been that same slight twist to the dagger protruding from the black cape Mohra had worn when she helped them escape from the steam pipes in the hold of the Bergenland.

"I can't swear to it," he said at last, "but I've got to admit that it does look something like it."

"I saw it very plainly," Kildare said, "and I would swear that this is either the same or one of a pair of identical daggers." His eyes gleamed triumphantly. "You see," he went on, "what I have been telling you is true. Mohra is an assistant of Wu Fang. Oh,

THE MYSTERIOUS WU FANG

I know it's hard to believe that such a beautiful creature is guilty of doing wrong, particularly when you're in love with her."

"Say, look here," Hazard blurted out.

Kildare chuckled and nudged him with his elbow. "Forget it," he said. "I didn't mean to hurt your feelings. I only wanted to warn you that I wouldn't be surprised if you meet the mysterious beauty again. My only suggestion is that you don't trust her."

THEN, BEFORE Hazard could think of an argument, he picked up the other instrument. It was the club he had wrested from their mysterious assailant. It was short, perhaps eight or ten inches in length, but very heavy.

"It must be loaded with lead," Hazard guessed.

Kildare shook his head. "No, it is made of a rare wood that grows only in the northern end of the Malay Peninsula. White people call it iron wood because of its hardness and weight. The Malays make clubs out of it exactly like this. It's so hard that it's difficult to cut even with steel. Nice little instrument isn't it?"

Hazard shuddered. "Nice. Why, that thing would crush a man's skull with just a slight blow."

"Exactly so," Kildare nodded.

"Gee," Cappy cut in, "that's what the cops here in New York ought to use."

Kildare passed it over to the boy.

"Maybe you would like to have it to remember tonight by," he said. "After all you saved me from being knocked on the head with it."

"Gee," Cappy breathed, "can I have it all for myself? Wait till I show it to my scout troop. Won't their eyes pop out!"

"Better not tell them just how you got it," Hazard suggested.

"Don't worry, I won't," Cappy answered. "I'll just tell them that a couple of swell guys gave it to me."

Kildare stared out through the blackness of the night. The streets were more dimly lighted now and narrower.

"We're getting there," he said. "A few more minutes and we'll be in the heart of Chinatown." A moment later, he shot an order to the driver. "Turn right here. Down Park Row." And again, a few minutes later—"Turn left. Let us out at the corner."

The taxi made the turn and drew up to the curb. They got out. "Now turn around and be ready to start at a moment's notice.

"Here." He handed the driver a five-dollar bill. "That's in case we should lose you before the night's over."

Then he led the way to a small dark alley. It was scarcely more than a two-foot passage leading back to a gloom that was impossible to penetrate with the human eye.

They slipped inside. For all they could tell, the passage might run for a hundred yards between these squalid buildings. But there was no sign of life whatever; it was as dark as pitch, narrow and foreboding. They stood there in the blackness, crouched against the damp stone walls.

"I think," Kildare hissed, "that the cab bearing Opporte will come down this street. It's the main entrance to Chinatown. Here comes one now. Wait!"

A cab cruised past slowly. As it went by they saw the license plate reflected in the tail light.

"No, that's not it," Kildare said.

Two minutes later, another cab passed. It was empty also and didn't have the right number.

They continued to watch through the rain-soaked, drizzling night. Then suddenly, all three grew tense. From somewhere nearby had come a whispering sound. It came in a singing high-pitched voice.

"Mr. Kildare."

Kildare turned quickly to Hazard.

"Did you hear that?" he demanded.

The reporter gave a short nod.

"Where did it come from?" Kildare asked.

"I don't know," Hazard answered. "It seemed to come from almost anywhere. From the street or the roof of one of these buildings or from the back of the alley. I—"

He stopped short, for through the inky blackness of the stinking alley, that whisper hissed again.

"Mr. Kildare."

Kildare turned his head now in utter astonishment. The faint sound did indeed come from everywhere in general and no place in particular. The very walls between which they stood vibrated with it.

Hazard fingered his automatic, brought it out of his pocket for instant action. A third time, the voice hissed, "Kildare." The short hairs along Hazard's spine were beginning to stand straight up. He shuddered as if from a sudden chill.

"How the devil does anybody know we're here?" Hazard asked in a hoarse, tense whisper.

"That," Kildare came back, "is the mystery of the East. Some things the Chinese do just don't make sense, but they do 'em."

The voice came again, this time nearer. So near, in fact, that Hazard jumped when he heard the hissed question—

"Kildare, you lookee for Wu Fang?"

"**GOOD LORD!**" Hazard gasped. "He's right on top of us."

"Shut up," Kildare snapped then, raising his voice so that it would carry back into the alley and upward—"Yes, I'm looking for Wu Fang. Know where he is?"

The answering whisper was low and almost inaudible.

"Me know. You come back alley. You see."

"It's a trap," Hazard hissed. "They'll get us in the back alley and then—"

"Sssh," Kildare cautioned with his lips at Hazard's ear. "Have your gun ready. We've got to take the chance. O.K, we're coming," he said aloud.

Turning he led the way into the inky blackness. Cappy followed close behind, clutching the club in his right hand. Hazard brought up the rear, with his automatic ready.

It was as though they were walking through a sea of ink. The light from the street lamp at the other end of the alley glowed dimly and the dismal rain suddenly cut off its feeble beams after they had penetrated the passage for perhaps ten feet.

Kildare stumbled over a heap of debris and nearly fell.

"Watch out for that junk," he cautioned.

"O.K.," Cappy said. "I found it."

141

Something rustled to the right; the boy ducked and his club came down, making a low, thwacking sound.

"Gee," he exclaimed. "I missed it."

"What was it?" Hazard breathed.

"A rat, I think."

"Let's hope so," Kildare countered.

They had gone perhaps a hundred feet when suddenly Kildare stopped and held out his hand to the others.

"Wait," he whispered. "It's a blind alley. We have come to the end."

"What do we do now?" Hazard gasped.

"We wait," Kildare answered. "We wait right here."

As those words came out, Hazard took a quick breath. He thought he could feel chilly fingers up along his back.

"I'm—I'm ready for anything," he declared. "If anything moves, I'll plug it."

He felt Kildare's arm on his. "Somebody's coming. Don't shoot, whatever you do. You may spoil our chances of finding what we're after."

Hazard listened. Yes, there was someone coming. He could hear a low shuffling of feet from inside one of the buildings that flanked the alley. Then they heard the scratching of metal against metal and next a hinge creaked ever so slightly.

A door was opening. No light shone through but there was a movement in the darkness at the side of the alley.

"Mr. Kildare."

"Right," Kildare hissed back.

"You will—come in?"

Kildare nodded and began feeling his way along the wall.

"Follow me," he whispered to the others as he found the door opening. He stepped inside. The door closed behind them and the whispered voice came once more.

"You look for Wu Fang, Mr. Kildare?"

"Yes," Kildare nodded. "How about a light?"

"Not yet, Mr. Kildare," answered the other in his singsong, Chinese voice. "First, we talk business. How much money you got?"

Kildare thought quickly, turned to Hazard.

"How much have you got?" he asked.

"Around seventy dollars."

"Good," Kildare nodded. "I've got a little better than fifty." He swung back to the Chinaman. "How about that? A hundred and twenty-five dollars. We'll give all we've got if you will show us where Wu Fang is."

The Chinaman hesitated.

"I've got a dollar and sixty-eight cents," Cappy cut in eagerly.

"You give me money," the Chinaman decided.

There was a general digging down in pockets and there in that pitch blackness where no one could see anyone else, they handed the money over to their invisible guide.

"You wait," said the Chinaman. "I be back." They heard the shuffling of feet followed by a door creaking.

Hazard started after him, but Kildare pulled him back.

"Wait," he cautioned. "You've got to handle these birds with kid gloves. It's a business with them. He's gone in where the

143

light is to count the money. He'll be back in a moment, see if he isn't."

Kildare was right. The Chinaman returned.

"O.K.?" Kildare demanded in a low voice.

"I show you," the Chinaman answered. "We must move in dark. You take hold my hand, Mr. Kildare. Hold on to the hands of most honorable assistants. You follow me."

"O.K.," Kildare nodded. "But get this, Charlie. If you double-cross us, I'll put a bullet in your head so quick you won't know what happened."

In that same singsong voice, the Chinaman hissed back, "You come."

That was a terrible experience, passing down rotten, creaking stairs, through long twisted corridors as black as night. There wasn't a light anywhere. The foul smells of underground Chinatown were mingled with that unmistakable, indescribable, Oriental tang of the East.

It seemed as though they had been walking for hours, strung out through narrow passages hand in hand, stumbling, feeling for their footing. And always when a question was asked of him, the Chinaman who led them merely hissed, "You come."

At length, Hazard said, "Say, we must be almost down to China itself by now. We've gone down enough creaking old stairs."

"We go upstairs now," the Chinaman answered. "I am stepping on first step."

That was true. They were climbing up a pair of strong steps. At the top, they reached another long, damp corridor.

THE CASE OF THE SIX COFFINS

The feeling was growing more and more strongly in Hazard that they were not entirely alone. It was a feeling that gave him the creeps, as though the sides of the pitch-black corridor through which they moved were lined with agents of Wu Fang who stood silent, letting them pass into a trap. But Kildare seemed hopefully confident.

For perhaps ten or fifteen minutes more, they walked through wide corridors. There could be no possible hope of finding their own way out of this mass of twining passages.

Suddenly, a door creaked ahead of them and they felt a blast of what seemed to be fresher air. Still, it was tinged even more strongly with the odor of the East, as though the smoke of incense had merged with the lotus blossom to form a rare and mysterious perfume.

They passed through the open doorway and stopped. Another door creaked open. Although they couldn't see a thing, they had the impression that they were in a room instead of a passage. They heard the slight shuffling sound of the Chinaman's feet. Then a door banged. Or was it two doors? They couldn't tell.

The two men were standing alone, not touching each other at all. Hazard heard Kildare exclaim, "He's gone!" Then a light flared in Kildare's hand as he struck a match.

The sputtering flame glowed brightly and showed them the interior of a stone room. There were no windows, and two doors in opposite walls. They were completely alone there in the chamber and they heard no sound from beyond those closed doors or the stone walls.

CHAPTER 15
TORTURE CHAMBER

BOTH MEN opened their mouths several times to ask each other questions, but closed them again as the horror of the situation crowded in on them.

Then Kildare ventured, "Maybe we're all right. I don't know. That Chinaman may have gone on to make sure everything was set for his escape after he shows us where Wu Fang is."

As he spoke, he was trying the door closest to him; it was a solid structure made of rock. Hazard turned back to the other door, began pounding on it.

"Cappy!" he shouted. "Oh, Cappy! Are you there?"

But the only reply he got was the echo of his voice against the four walls of the tightly sealed vault.

"It's my guess," Kildare said, "that the Chinaman took Cappy with him. It all happened so quickly in the dark. I felt the Chinaman slip away and at the same time, I felt Cappy's hand slip out of mine."

"Yes," Hazard said, "I was holding his other hand and the kid left me just as we stopped."

The match spluttered and went out. Kildare lighted others and in their pale, flickering glow, he and Hazard studied first one door and then another. They pushed hard against each of them, but they remained immovable.

"Maybe," Hazard said, "the two of us could rush one of these doors and break it open."

"I doubt it," Kildare replied, shaking his head. "Our best bet is to wait until something turns up. At least, we've got our automatics; that gives us a fair chance of getting out alive."

But Hazard wasn't worrying about himself now. He was thinking about Cappy. "I wish I knew where the kid is," he breathed.

"He's a clever youngster," Kildare decided. "He'll get by."

As he talked, he began to light more matches and made an inspection of the stone walls. He rapped the ceiling with his fist.

"It's a vault sure enough," he said. "Look at this ceiling. It's made out of one solid slab of pavement stone. Listen!" The room grew instantly silent. "Hear anything?"

Hazard shook his head. "Not a thing. Lord, it's like a tomb in here."

"That may be the general idea," Kildare said. "Why the devil doesn't the Chinaman come back? Why don't we hear from Cappy?"

Minutes dragged on. They stood there, listening. Over head, they thought they heard faint shuffling sounds, but they couldn't be sure.

"What do you expect to hear?" Hazard demanded. His nerves were rapidly approaching the breaking point.

Kildare shrugged. "I don't know. It was just an idea that popped into my mind when I saw the paving stone. There's no telling how thick that ceiling might be. Perhaps it's the paving stone of a sidewalk. All of Chinatown is honeycombed with rooms and passages. I have known cases where families were found living underground, practicing some sort of evil, whose kids grew to be ten or twelve year olds before they ever got out to see the light of day."

Hazard shuddered.

Kildare was moving slowly along one of the two blank walls now. He put out the match he was holding as the flame neared his fingers and struck another one. Then, by the flickering light he bent down to examine a tiny niche.

Hazard joined him. His eyes bulged and his voice was husky as he asked, "Find anything?"

Kildare pointed. "Just this crack," he said. "It's large enough for a small rat to get through and seems to go quite deep in the wall. It may extend through to the other side."

Suddenly, with his free hand, he started gathering up small chips of stone which he proceeded to pack in the crevice.

"At least," he said grimly, "Wu Fang won't be able to send his little murder beasts through that as long as those stones stay there."

Hazard gave a start and his heart began pounding away up in the back of his head like the beating of a great drum. Cold sweat poured out on his forehead. "Wu Fang!" he exclaimed. "What makes you think Wu Fang knows we are here?"

Kildare shrugged. "You can't tell what that Chinaman will do. For all we know it may have been Wu Fang himself who led us here—although I doubt it. It didn't sound like his voice."

"Good Lord!" said Hazard. "Wu Fang wouldn't stoop to taking a hundred and some odd dollars as a bribe. He wouldn't bother with a thing like that."

"Oh, I don't know," Kildare replied. "It would certainly be a convincing way to turn our suspicions away from him. If that was a trick to get us here, you've got to admit it was pretty clever."

"Damnably clever," Hazard rasped. He gave a start as the match Kildare had been holding went out.

"For the love of heaven," he hissed in the pitch blackness, "light another match, will you? I'll go nuts if I have to stay in this darkness, not knowing what's going to happen."

"Sorry, old man," Kildare said, "it was the last match I had. Have you any?"

WITH FRANTIC desperation, Hazard began fumbling in his pockets. Panic seized him now as his hands came out—empty. He went the rounds again, probing the bottoms of all the pockets in his coat. Suddenly, he let out a triumphant cry.

"Here, I've got some. You'd better take them. My hands aren't any too steady. Damn it! Why doesn't something happen!"

He even jumped when his hand touched Kildare's in the darkness. He heard Kildare flip open the top of the paper book of matches, then heard Kildare's voice. "There's only one here."

"Maybe," Hazard ventured, "we could build a fire. I've got a couple of hunks of paper in my pocket."

"No," Kildare countered instantly, "that would only burn out the oxygen in this room sooner. I don't think we're getting any ventilation in here. If that damn Chinaman has sold us to Wu Fang for a higher price, we may be left here the rest of our lives to rot—although I can't quite figure Wu Fang letting us off so easily."

"Then," Hazard said, "we're going to sit here in the dark and wait for something to happen?"

"Yes," Kildare answered in a low voice. "I'm going to hold this match ready to strike if something does happen. It may be just the one light that will help us shoot our way out of danger."

Minutes passed, then Hazard caught Kildare's arm, pinched it savagely.

"Listen!" he hissed. "What's that? There's a sound coming from the other side of that door. Not the one that we entered, but the other one. I think the Chinaman went out that way."

They stood tense, their muscles tightening, ready for instant action.

"Yes," Kildare agreed. "They're at the door now."

A bolt slid back; it creaked as the iron bar moved through the slots.

"Have your gun ready," Kildare whispered. "If anything happens that doesn't seem just right, I'll strike the match. Be ready to shoot, but watch out. Cappy may be with him. Don't hit the kid."

Hazard squared himself before the door, which was now opening. He heard footsteps, but no one spoke for the first few seconds. *Step, step, step.* In the pitch blackness they could see nothing.

Hazard sensed that more than one person was entering. *Step, shuffle, step.* It sounded very much like a man with a limp, a man who dragged one foot. Kildare's voice rang out, low and commanding—

"Who's there?"

In answer, the voice of the Chinaman who had led them to the room came back, "Everything all right. You come. Where is your hand?"

Hazard stepped close to Kildare.

"Listen," he hissed, "there's somebody else in this room besides that Chinaman. Two or three men came in. Light the—"

But he got no farther. Strong arms like bands of steel seized him suddenly from behind. A heavy hand was clapped over his mouth and his automatic was pinned at his side.

"The match won't light," Kildare cracked. "It's a dud. Try—" His words broke off in a smothered cry. Smothered, Hazard guessed, by similar means to those that had cut off his words.

Suddenly, a crash sounded, a great, ringing crash. Then the space about him seemed brightly illuminated with stars dancing before him in every direction. The faint sound of a struggle, the boom of a gun, and then total unconsciousness flooded over him.

WHEN HAZARD opened his eyes, he was in a dimly lighted room. Vague figures were grouped about. Then he heard Kildare's voice from somewhere behind him.

"You vile, inhuman, yellow devil," Kildare was rasping.

Hazard's brain cleared and he took in everything in one horrified glance. The room was large, and lighted by indirect means. He and Kildare were sitting on heavy teakwood chairs— were bound to them, in fact, with stout ropes. A teak-wood table, the top of which rose stomach-high, was in front of them.

Beyond the table stood Wu Fang. He stood there with his talon-like hands clasped before him on his heavy, yellow robe which extended to the floor in silken folds. His jade-green eyes were gleaming iridescently and his thin, cruel lips were smiling. Behind him was an immense gilt idol. Rich, dark draperies entirely covered the walls.

All of this Hazard took in at a glance, but the sight that struck him with horror, so that his eyes bulged from his head and his blood chilled, were the two figures to the right.

Except for the scantiest of underclothing, they were naked. There was a young man and a young woman. They were fastened in such a position that each seemed to be standing on a small wheel, their hands were tied over their heads to another wheel above. The two wheels were placed far enough apart so that each body was stretched straight at full length. The wheels were turning ever so slowly in opposite directions from each other. In this manner, the bodies of the girl and the man were being horribly twisted.

The man was George Opporte. He still wore his horn-rimmed glasses. And the girl—he had watched that lovely, slim body walk down the deck of the Bergenland. She was still conscious and her eyes were wide and terror-stricken. They were fixed upon Hazard. There was pleading in those eyes, but the lovely lips were silent.

The twisting machine moved on. The wheels turned so slowly that their motion could scarcely be noted with the eye. Opporte let out a terrific screech of pain; his whole body was trembling with the anguish of the torture. But Mohra's lips never moved.

Hazard gasped her name, "Mohra!"

He saw a hurt look come into those lovely dark eyes.

Then suddenly, Wu Fang chuckled. It wasn't an unkind chuckle; an almost paternal look came into his eyes as he uttered it. His laughter seemed more like the mirth of a kindly old family doctor recounting the antics of some child patient.

"Ah," he said. "It is too bad that we all must have the bitter with the sweet. You see before you a very beautiful young woman. It has become known to me that she was the instrument of your escape from the steam pipes in the hold of the Bergenland. So—" he shrugged—"she is now receiving the beginning of her punishment. The end?" He shrugged again. "That depends upon my will. The other one you know, of course. I believe you were talking with him when my agents had his friend call him to his assistance."

Jerry Hazard had stood all he could.

"You damned yellow swine," he burst forth. "If I could get out of this chair, I'd tear your heart out with my bare hands. I'll get you for this if I have to come back from hell to do it."

Wu Fang's long-fingernailed hands clasped each other more closely in a gesture of pleasure and his smile now was even more benign than it had been before.

"That's a very noble thought, Mr. Hazard," he purred. "You are brave to think of such a thing. But perhaps it is more chivalry than bravery. You have become very much enamored with the beauty of this girl. Even I can understand that, I whom you call a yellow swine."

His smile broadened. "But even a swine has natural feelings and passions like other animals."

Hazard was straining frantically at the ropes that bound him.

"No use," Kildare told him. "Save your strength. You're tied up plenty tight. We're at the mercy of this yellow devil."

Mohra uttered a little cry. Her face was ghastly white now. Then a shudder passed through her and her twisted body went limp, her head dropping forward on her chest.

"Now, it is my turn for complete triumph," Wu Fang said. "I have lived for this moment, gentlemen, that I might even up a little score between you and me, Mr. Kildare. Hazard, as your assistant, will go the same way."

He turned to a drape that covered one wall, uttered two words:

"Troll! Troll!" The drapery moved slightly. "You may come out."

Hazard's horror-stricken eyes were searching the room when he heard Kildare gasp, "Merciful God!" It was a frantic prayer.

CHAPTER 16
THREE STRANGE VISITORS

KILDARE'S EYES were glued to the bottom edge of the drapery. Hazard followed his gaze and a gasp escaped his lips.

"The stomach chewers!" he yelled.

Two tiny animals were running across the floor toward Wu Fang. They were both alike, about five inches in length from the tip of their pointed, murderous noses to the ends of their tails.

Both men had seen an animal like that before, when Kildare had shot it on to the deck of the Bergenland.

Wu Fang was chuckling as the animals drew near him. When they had nearly reached him, he thrust out a short stick on the end of which was a piece of cloth. He waved it in front of him, and, as though it were a wand of magic, the little beasts suddenly stopped short.

"Climb up on the table," Wu Fang commanded.

The animals obeyed instantly. Each climbed up a table leg and perched on the top, opposite from the side where Kildare and Hazard sat.

"You will stay there," Wu Fang commanded. "I see, gentlemen," he went on, "that you recognize my little agents of the most painful death in my power. You saw one, I believe, leaving the stateroom of Mr. Kitchner who was, I regret to say, killed by mistake."

The little beasts were squatting now on their lizard-like hind legs. Suddenly, Wu Fang unclasped his long-nailed hands and clapped them twice. The sounds rang out in the low, vaulted room like pistol shots. Immediately, a figure entered through some doorway that the two prisoners hadn't noticed. He was dark-skinned and large framed. His arms were very long and hung down at his sides like the arms of an ape.

Wu Fang spoke to him in a low voice. The man nodded, then advanced toward Kildare. With a quick movement, he tore the clothing from his stomach so that the skin showed bare; then moved to Hazard. But before he could touch him, Hazard tried to leap up in the chair. Half insane with rage, his head darted forward and before the dark-skinned servant could draw back he had sunk his teeth deep into the flesh of the man's arm. The servant's other arm flashed through the air and his big, paw-like hand struck a stinging

A slot opened and a man looked out.

blow on the side of the reporter's head. The terrific force of the blow sent Hazard's head reeling. When his brain cleared, the slave had bared his stomach also and had vanished from the room.

"Now," Wu Fang smiled, "I believe we are ready for my little murder agents."

He waved the stick behind the little beasts. They turned, stared for a moment with their noses twitching; then they fled across the top of the table toward Kildare and Hazard.

"Stop!" called Wu Fang.

The little beasts had reached the brink of the table. If they had kept on they would have leaped across the foot of space that separated them from the bared stomachs of the two men.

Hazard was doubled over in his chair as much as his ropes

THE CASE OF THE SIX COFFINS

They began talking in Chinese.

would permit. Kildare cringed. The faces of both men were ashen white.

Kildare lashed out with, "Wu Fang, remember this. You are attacking a Federal man and his agent. You are going to kill us. I haven't a doubt about that, and we are powerless to stop you now. But remember this: Someone is going to hunt you down and finish you off for this and you're other crimes. The murder of a Federal investigator has never yet gone un-avenged."

Wu Fang stood there chuckling, clasping and unclasping his yellow hands.

"And while you are speaking of not forgetting, my friend," he said softly, "it might be well for you to remember something too—a cablegram from your department. You received it at London, and it informed you that you are no longer a Federal agent. You are merely a private citizen who has taken the law into his own hands. I admit, of course, that it was one of my agents who arranged for your dismissal from the department. But that, therefore, makes no difference now. All that matters now, Mr. Kildare, is that I am killing a private citizen, not a Federal agent. I am merely disposing of a pest who has crossed my path too many times and I am also doing away with a meddlesome, snooping newspaper man who would not give me the publicity which I deserve."

He straightened his stooped, narrowed shoulders and raised the stick.

At this instant the attention of Kildare and Hazard was snatched from the pinched yellow face of Wu Fang. The startled look in their eyes must have been apparent to the Dragon Lord for be suddenly stopped short.

There, behind Wu Fang, above the head of the great gilt idol something had moved. It was a small head and a small pair of shoulders. It was Cappy, and he was carrying the black ironwood club in his upraised hand.

The only thing that saved Wu Fang from having his skull crushed in was the sudden change of expression in the faces of the two men before him. The change was only slight, but it was enough to warn him.

WU FANG whirled with astonishing speed. Cappy leaped for him, the club ready to descend. Then the mysterious light which had illuminated the place suddenly went out and they were in total darkness.

The blackness was accompanied by a wild bedlam of sound. Wu Fang's voice rasped out, shouting an order in the same strange tongue he had used in addressing his half-naked servant. There was a terrific rumble, as of great wheels rolling over stone pavement mingled with the penetrating shrill of a police whistle.

Hazard heard something creeping beside him on the floor. Kicking with all his might, his toes braced against the floor, he flung the chair to which he was bound over backward. He fell sidewise, just as something small and scaly leaped past him. A tiny light blinked like the flame of a match. Then it went out. He heard the tramp of heavy feet.

Next, he felt the ropes about him grow loose and he was shaking them off as the boy cut his bindings in the pitch blackness.

A door burst open from somewhere. There were shouts, dancing flashlights illuminated the room. In the shifty light of an electric torch, Hazard saw Cappy cutting the ropes that bound Kildare to his chair.

"The beasts," Kildare exclaimed, "those lizard things. Where are they? Kill them before they get somebody."

"I got one," Cappy snapped back. "I think the other one got away."

"What the devil is going on here, anyhow?" a booming voice demanded.

They were completely surrounded by police.

"Listen," Kildare cracked, talking fast and pulling his clothing together in front of him. "I am Kildare, Federal investigator." He flashed his badge. "Wu Fang is in here somewhere. Cut down that man and woman before—"

He pointed to where Mohra and Opporte had been trussed up in the torture machine.

"Good Lord!" he breathed. "They're gone! There's nothing there!"

"What's happened?" the lieutenant in charge of the raiders demanded. "Do you know what you're talking about?"

"Of course," Kildare snapped. "Let me take your light. I'll show you."

One of the police officers handed him a flashlight. He turned it back across the room toward the spot where Opporte and Mohra had hung. A strange, puzzled look came into his face.

"Why, they were right over there," he said.

Hazard was beside him, pointing in the direction that the beam of light had taken.

"Look!" he exclaimed. "This room is only half the size that it was before."

Kildare groaned and nodded.

"Yes," he said. "I remember now. That rumbling sound we heard after the lights went out must have been the noise of that stone slab coming down and cutting the room in two." He whirled to the police officers. "They're behind that wall," he said. "Wu Fang is there. All of his agents are down here under the ground somewhere. We've got to—"

He darted out of the door through which the police had entered, a door behind where he and Kildare had been sitting. There was a wild search of the underground passages. Flashlights blinked everywhere. Locked doors were burst open. But nothing was revealed, no sign of Wu Fang, no sign of Mohra.

Suddenly, Kildare rushed back to the police lieutenant.

"We've got to leave," he told him. "There's a house uptown that I'm afraid holds a ghastly secret. You take charge here and search the whole of Chinatown if you have to get these devils.

Well go up there and try to forestall any attempt to steal Opporte's secret."

The lieutenant gave a short nod.

"Right," he said. "I don't know what you're talking about, but I've got a description of Wu Fang and you say there's a girl with him?"

"Yes," Kildare answered. "A white girl with dark hair. She may be a Turk or an Afghan. She's dark and very beautiful. Wu Fang also has George Opporte, the inventor. I'm going to Opporte's house now. Get in touch with you later."

EVENTUALLY THE three—Kildare, Hazard and Cappy—found their way to the street. As the taxi drove them uptown Kildare faced the boy.

"Young man," he said. "It seems to me this night is filled with commendations for your work. But there are some things need explanation. What happened to you after you and the Chinaman vanished from the room?"

Cappy grinned.

"Well, sir," he said, "I don't know what made me do it, Mr. Kildare, but I got sort of an idea that Chinaman was going to do something funny. The minute we stopped, I slid around, let go of your hand and Jerry's and followed him. I just got through the door behind him when he shut it and bolted it. Then I knew something was wrong. So I followed him down the passage on tiptoe. Once he stopped. Perhaps he had heard me. I didn't even breathe then. Gee, I was scared, but I kept the club that you gave me ready to sock him with if something happened. We kept going in the dark until we came to a door at the end of a long, twisting passage. Gee, it was scary. You ought to have been there, Jerry."

"Thanks," Hazard said dryly, "I've had about enough scary things for one night. You sure had nerve with you, kid, to follow through."

"Well, gee, I had to," Cappy explained. "I didn't dare get scared and run. I didn't know where I was going anyway. Then we came to this door and the Chinaman knocked. I think it was three times—or maybe four. A slot in the door opened and a man looked out. It was the same man who was threatening you with those lizards or rats or whatever they were on the table."

"That," Kildare said, "was Wu Fang."

"Gee," Cappy breathed, his eyes popping wide open. "Well, anyway, he began talking to the Chinaman. They talked in Chinese and I couldn't tell what they were saying until I heard 'Mr. Kildare.'"

"The yellow rat!" rasped Kildare. "You see, Hazard? It was just about as I guessed. He got all the money from us that he could and then went to Wu Fang and tried to sell us over to him."

"Yes, sir," Cappy nodded. "I guess that was it because they were arguing about something and the Chinaman got awful mad. Then Wu Fang said something in English. He said it didn't matter because he wouldn't live to get back to you. Then he threw something through the door. It looked like a rat.

"I saw it jump at the Chinaman and I thought it was going to jump at me, too. I hit it with my club just as Wu Fang closed

162

the slot in the door. I killed it. The Chinaman didn't know I was with him until then. Then he grabbed me.

"He let out some awful yells and ran down the passage, dragging me after him. When we got around the corner, he told me I had saved his life by killing that—he called it by some Chinese name I can't remember. He said Wu Fang was a something. I guess that was in Chinese, too. It sounded like an awful name, anyway—and he said because I had saved him he would lead me to Wu Fang's place. He showed me how to get to that room where you were tied and then he ran away. He said he was going to call the police."

Kildare studied the boy for a moment.

"Cappy," he said at length, "I have been on Wu Fang's trail for quite some time; and this is the first occasion I have known him to bungle. He certainly made a mistake by not paying that Chinaman for turning us over to him."

"But listen," Hazard cut in, "wasn't it the same Chinaman who came back afterward with the thugs and told us to follow him?"

Kildare shook his head.

"Apparently not. It must have been one of Wu Fang's agents impersonating him."

He settled back in the seat of the taxi.

"Well," he said, "that fixes things more clearly in my mind. I wonder what we'll find at Opporte's house. I'm going to get the surprise of my life if Wu Fang's agents haven't been there already."

KILDARE WASN'T surprised for when they left the taxi

and walked up the drive through the pelting rain, the officer who was on guard in the alcove of the main entrance stepped out briskly, gun in hand.

"Things all right, officer?" Kildare asked. "I'm back here with my two assistants. What's happened since that scream earlier this evening? What did you find there?"

"That's a funny thing," the officer said. "We didn't find anything. We couldn't even find the woman who had screamed. We searched two or three buildings from top, but didn't find a soul who knew any more about it than we did. Then we came back here and—"

"And you found the house vacant," Kildare cut in. "Good Lord, man, don't you know that scream was a blind? You were sent here to watch this house and nothing else."

"Well, I'm sorry, sir," said the cop, "but a woman screaming for help in the night and especially a night like this—"

Kildare nodded quickly. "Yes," he said, "I know. I guess almost anyone would have done the same thing under the circumstances. What's happened since you got back?"

"Well, sir," the cop answered, "three things happened. There's three of us on this job, one at the back door and two at the front. I'm here at the main entrance and there's a man down at the service entrance below. First there was a man came, he said he had to talk to Mr. Opporte on something very important, so I went into the house to tell Opporte, and it was then I remembered the house was empty. Funny, too. While I was in there, I heard somebody run up the stairs and then I heard a window going up. I did some tall searching, I don't mind telling you. I looked over every room, but I couldn't find a thing. Even the window that I had heard going up had been pulled back down again. There wasn't anybody in the house, not a soul, so I told the man that had called to see Opporte that he wasn't in. He thanked me and left."

"What did he look like?" Kildare asked. "Did you get a look at him?"

"Well, he was about five feet ten," the cop answered. "He wore a raincoat, so I couldn't see just how he was dressed, but he spoke with an accent, maybe Italian or French or Spanish. He was very polite. About an hour later I heard Flannigan— that's the man at the back door—blow his whistle and Mike and I came running around from the front of the house and would you believe it sir, something was crawling up the side of the house right out of the alley! At least, I think it did. Flannigan swears he saw it. It climbed just as good as a monkey could any day. I shot at it and it dropped. When it struck the alley, it ran like a man."

"Did you get it?" Kildare demanded.

"No, sir," said the cop. "He got away."

Kildare frowned.

"But how could he get away?" he asked. "You had the alley blocked, didn't you, on each end?"

"Yes, sir," the officer nodded. "I think he got in a cellar window of the next house. We left Flannigan to watch the alley and Mike and I went in the house and searched it, but we couldn't find him anywhere.

"About an hour after that, we got a call from headquarters.

At least, that's what they said. They said they had a riot call and needed everybody on the force. They wanted us to come down right away. It sounded kind of fishy to me after this screaming woman business, so I rang headquarters back. They said they didn't know anything about it."

Kildare nodded slowly. "O.K., officer. Here's what you do next. You and Flannigan and Mike, all three of you, go away. The house is being watched, and I want you to make as much show of leaving as possible. Is there a passage that leads through from the street to the back of the house?"

"Yes, sir," the cop nodded.

"Very well," Kildare went on. "Slip through the house now while I'm standing here and unlock the back door from the inside. The three of us are going to leave. Give us five minutes start and then you go out on the sidewalk, call Mike and Flannigan in a loud voice and tell them that you have orders to report at headquarters. Get them together and walk down the street.

"Go back to headquarters in case someone is trailing you. Then return by another route. There's an all-night lunch counter over on the corner of the avenue. Go in there and keep one man posted at the corner."

The cop looked at him strangely.

"But," he ventured, "I thought you wanted this house watched. It will be left alone that way."

"Not if we slip in the back door, it won't," Kildare smiled. "You stay at the lunch counter and keep one man posted to listen for my whistle. The three of us are going to come back through the back door. I would like, if possible, to corner both this mysterious climber and the man with the foreign accent."

The cop nodded.

"Yes, sir," he said. "I get you. And I wish you luck. It's kind of spooky inside that house, sir. It gave me the creeps, just standing out here with my gun even. I never saw anything that could climb like that guy could. It ain't human."

CHAPTER 17
HOUSE OF CORPSES

KILDARE, HAZARD and Cappy walked down the steps out into the driving rain again.

"This is certainly a lovely night for murders," Hazard shivered. "That wind must be blowing forty miles an hour and it's still rising. I think we will have a thunderstorm about midnight."

With heads bowed to fight the biting wind they struggled toward the avenue, a distance of less than a half block. They stopped at the corner in full view of the whole cross-town street and hailed a cruising cab.

"Up two blocks," Kildare said when they had gotten inside.

The driver drove two blocks.

"Now turn right," Kildare said, and after that block was passed, "turn right again and then take the next right."

He slipped a dollar bill into the chauffeur's hand as he ordered him to stop in the middle of the block. The driver looked at him strangely.

"Get out of this section as quick as you can," Kildare ordered, "and forget about this. Do you understand?"

The driver nodded. "Yes sir."

The trio slipped into an alley that ran between the houses, climbed a fence noiselessly and then were in the backyard of the Opporte house. Bent over and moving without a sound, they reached the kitchen door.

Kildare pushed it open easily, held it ajar for the others to follow, then locked it.

"So far, so good," he breathed. "Now, let's see. There's a light in the laboratory and the living room-office. I think we'll leave them on and avoid those rooms. No, wait here, Cappy."

As they walked past a dark doorway, something brushed his arm. It was a heavy drape that hung from a curtain pole.

"There, son," he said. "Throw that over you. You're small and I think you can get away with it. Besides, the lights in those rooms are rather dim. I want you to slip around under the windows and look at each one to be sure it's fastened securely. Don't show yourself in front of a window unless it's unlocked and you have to fasten it."

"Yes sir," Cappy nodded.

The two men waited at the open doorway while the little fellow glided into the lighted room silently, moving on his hands and knees beneath the dark curtain. He reached one window, rose up against the side wall and examined it. Apparently, that was locked. He moved to the next and the next and then to the laboratory.

After ten minutes, he came back.

"They're all locked, sir," he said.

"Good," Kildare nodded. "I'll take the curtain back where I found it."

When he had done that, he made a tour of the downstairs windows in the rooms that were not lighted.

"Everything is locked up tight down here on the first floor," he said. "Now we'll go up to the second floor."

The carpeted stairs creaked a little as they moved up step by step. Suddenly, he stopped.

"Damn the luck!" he said. "I forgot. Our guns are gone. They took them when they knocked us out in Chinatown. Well, well have to get along without them."

"Do you want my club?" Cappy asked.

"Yes," Kildare decided. "Do you mind if I borrow it for this occasion?"

The boy slipped the ironwood stick into his hand. The second floor was in total darkness. They made a tour of all the windows and found them locked except one on the side. Hazard frowned in deep thought and started inspecting the glass.

"How the devil," he ventured, "do you suppose that climber knew this window was unlocked? I'll bet this is the one he was headed for."

Kildare pushed him back. "Keep away. Don't show yourself right in the window. Stand behind the curtains."

Very slowly, he moved his hand to the lock and latched it.

"Now well take a look around the third floor," he said.

They found five windows unlocked on that floor. All of them looked on to the alley.

"Good Lord!" Hazard breathed. "It's uncanny."

"Yes," Kildare nodded. "Let's see," he went on. "There's only one staircase. That means that if we hide on the second floor, we ought to nab anyone coming down."

He led the way to the second floor and there in the darkness, they crouched.

IN SPITE of the cozy warmth of the house, a cold, clammy feeling began creeping over Hazard as he squatted there against the wall. The storm outside had risen in violence. Lightning flashed and thunder bellowed in the night. It seemed that all the horrible things in the world were suddenly let loose out there in the darkness.

From whence would come the agent of Wu Fang for whom they were lying in wait? Something creaked. Hazard tensed.

"It sounds like someone on the stairs," Cappy whispered.

"I think," Kildare hissed back, "it's a shutter. Wait! There it is again."

The sound was very faint and low. Then suddenly, all three of them jumped as a crash of thunder, greater than any that had sounded before, bellowed down from the storm-torn skies and the lightning illuminated the hallway almost as brightly as daylight.

The next second, as though some gigantic power had seized the building, the air was filled with a low moan. The house shuddered as though the very structure itself were tortured with fear.

Whoooooo! The very floor on which they crouched shivered under them. Cappy clutched Hazard's arm.

In the lightning flash they saw a heavy, half-naked man carrying a ghastly human burden.

"Holy Gee," he breathed. "What is it, ghosts?"

Hazard fought to keep his calm.

"No," he answered in a whisper, "not ghosts. Ssh! Something's coming."

The moaning was increasing in volume. Suddenly, it died for an instant. Then, almost directly over their heads, they heard a thud. It came ever so gently as though a pair of bare feet had dropped a short distance to a carpeted floor.

There was a tense moment of listening. A clap of thunder, then wind, and with that terrific blast, came the moaning sound again. Now it was stronger than ever.

It seemed they could hear nothing else no matter how hard they listened. Then the moaning died away. Stillness. A slight creak of a step above them. A great clock somewhere in a steeple began clanging: Eight nine, ten, eleven, twelve.

Crash! The heavens were split wide open with that blast of thunder. Lightning blinked through the windows, silhouetting them against the wall.

Kildare tensed. "I've got it," he said. "Someone came through the skylight and left it open. The wind is blowing across the opening—maybe."

Hazard's eyes were glued to the railing. With a sudden, convulsive movement, he clutched Kildare's arm, and as he pointed, they were swallowed in total darkness again.

The stairs in front of them creaked softly. Someone was coming down.

Hazard's flesh seemed to be rising up from his muscles. He felt a tingling sensation along his backbone as though his hair were standing on end. If only that lightning didn't blink now, and reveal their presence to the climber.

Creak, creak, creak!

A shadow came into view, then in the very dim reflection from the street lamp outside, they saw a form—a great, huge and stooped form. It stood bent over. Or was it carrying a burden?

The figure was coming toward them rapidly now. They had

the advantage at the moment because they were crouched in the darkness of the hall beside the stair rail. They could hear feet gently brushing the thick carpet. The figure was almost opposite, scarcely four feet from them.

Blam! A crash of thunder sounded and the lightning blasted. At the same time, Kildare let out a blood-curling yell and leaped up, club in hand.

In the flash they saw him strike at a heavy, partially clad man who carried over one shoulder the body of another human being. As the lightning blinked and went out again, there was a wild scramble. The intruder dropped his burden.

There was a thwacking sound as of a club coming down on a skull. Then a pounding as several bodies tumbled down the stairs to the first floor.

Hazard had been kicked back by the bare feet of the prowler, striking him in the face. It stunned him for an instant. Now he was rushing down the stairs, three steps at a time. He heard Kildare shout something.

"The lights! Turn on the lights!" Hazard stumbled toward the switch, flipped it on. The lower hall was flooded with illumination. There were three forms on the floor. Two of them were still. The third was Kildare. He was picking himself up; the short, ironwood club, one end damp with blood, was clutched tightly in his right hand.

Hazard stared down at the other two forms. One was the body of the night climber. He was powerful, long-armed, much like the servant of Wu Fang who had bared their stomachs for the attack of the poison beasts. There was a soft, bloody spot on the back of his head where the club had crushed the thick skull.

The other figure—Hazard gasped in amazement when he saw it.

"It's Opporte!" he yelled. "Look!"

Opporte's body was lying twisted on the floor in a pool of blood. His mouth was open, but no tongue was there. His arms ended in horrible red-smeared stubs where the hands bad been chopped off at the wrists. His eyes were partially closed.

They bent down over him instantly.

"He's still alive," Kildare breathed in horror. "But Wu Fang has fixed him so he can't tell us anything, either by word of mouth or by the written word. He has chopped off his hands and cut off his tongue. The devil!"

Then, as though Opporte had heard Kildare's words, his eyes opened with a great effort. They were pleading eyes. His mouth moved in a ghastly effort to speak, but no words came out.

"He's trying to say something," Hazard gasped.

"Go to it, man," Kildare said. "Can't you find some way?"

"Look!" Cappy exclaimed. "His foot! His right foot is moving! See it? He's trying to talk with his foot."

Cappy dived down by the foot of the prostrate man, held his hand so that the toe touched his fingers.

"I've got it," he said. "He's trying to talk in code."

Kildare groaned. "Who knows code?"

"I do," Cappy declared. "It's the international code that they use in wireless. I learned it in the Boy Scout troop. Wait!"

While he crouched at the foot of the inventor and spelled

the words aloud, Kildare bound up the stubs of the arms in a frantic effort to stop the flow of blood.

As Cappy uttered the letters that Opporte was tapping out, Hazard wrote them down.

WU FANG MADE—TELL—FORMULA TOO LONG—REMEMBER. MARCUS DARIEN HAS IT. AWARDED ME—DARIEN PRIZE—SORRY—

CHAPTER 18
WINGS OF TERROR

WITH THAT last tapping of his foot, George Opporte's fight for life seemed to be over. He made one last effort to stare at the boy who was recording his message, as if he would like to read it to be sure it had been translated correctly. But his eyes glazed and his body relaxed.

Kildare made a hasty examination.

"Dead, poor fellow," he said after a moment. "Bled to death. What's the message, Hazard?"

"It's terrible," Hazard answered. "Look!"

He held out the slip of paper. Kildare's eyes flashed over the words.

"Quick!" he said. "We've got to beat Wu Fang to Darien's house. Do you know where he lives?"

Hazard nodded. "I interviewed him one time. It's on Park Avenue."

When they were in a taxi, speeding to the palatial home of

Marcus Darien, Hazard recited the history of the Darien prize again.

"It seems," he said, "that this man Darien owns one of the richest diamond mines in the world. He's a philanthropist and is particularly interested in promoting peace because he lost his only son in the war. Each year, as you know, he offers a prize of a million dollars for the most deadly war instrument invented during the previous year. The final awards are usually made secretly. I knew Opporte had been mentioned for the prize but I didn't know the award had actually been made until just now.

"The stipulation, of course, is that the inventor turn over formula, samples—everything, to him. Darien offers such an enormous prize so that the inventor can live a life of ease, and will not be tempted to accept, from then on, other offers. Darien, I believe, puts the formulas and samples in a tight vault or else destroys them entirely."

Kildare groaned. He stared at the message again, the message that Opporte had tapped out with his foot just before he died.

"Opporte told Wu Fang that he had given the formula to Darien," he said. "Well, we'll stop Wu Fang from getting that formula if we can."

"What do you think he will do with it when he gets it?" Hazard asked. For a sort of premonition was creeping over him. It seemed inevitable that the all-powerful Wu Fang would get that formula.

"What do you mean, when he gets it?" Kildare snapped. "We can't let him get it. We've got to stop him."

Hazard nodded hopefully. "Sure, if we can, but it seems almost an impossibility to stop that fiend from doing anything he wants to."

"Don't forget," Kildare reminded him. "Wu Fang has slipped on two details now. First, he slipped up by not paying that Chinaman guide to double-cross us and now, more recently, he's slipped because he let Opporte live long enough to tell us what happened. Now we've got to make Wu Fang slip up once more. We've got to get him this time."

The car drew up before a massive residence that occupied nearly a whole block. Kildare, Hazard and Cappy piled out, ran up the steps. It was well after midnight and they had to wait several minutes to get an answer to their insistent ringing.

At last a butler with side-burns and a bath robe wrapped around him opened the door as far as the chain lock would permit and scowled out at them.

"Yes sir," he said. "What's wanted?"

Kildare flashed his badge. "We've got to see Mr. Marcus Darien at once," he snapped.

The butler shook his head and started to close the door.

"I'm sorry, sir, but he's not at home. He has left town."

"Left town!"

"Yes, sir. More than a day ago."

"Where did he go?" Kildare asked.

"He's—well, blast it all," the butler suddenly exploded, "do I have to tell everybody who comes where Mr. Darien has gone?"

Kildare's hand flashed through the crack in the door; he caught the butler firmly by the front of his bath robe and pulled him close to the opening.

"Listen," he exclaimed, "has someone been here ahead of us, asking for Mr. Darien?"

The butler looked frightened. "Yes sir," he said.

"What sort of a man was he and how long ago did he come?"

"I didn't get a good look at him," the butler said. "He was a fair-sized man, I should say, and came from some department or other. He had a badge like yours that he showed me."

"And you told him Darien had gone?"

"Yes sir. He came about two or possibly three hours ago, sir. I was just retiring then. I told him as I will tell you now that Mr. Darien left on his yacht for South America."

Kildare groaned.

"What's the name of the yacht?"

"I know," Hazard cut in. "It's The Nordic."

"That's right, sir," the butler nodded. "And now if you don't mind, I'll go back to my sleep, sir."

"Just one more question," Kildare shot back at him, still holding him at the crack in the door. "Mr. Darien gave a prize a short time ago to George Opporte for a deadly instrument of war. Do you know whether he took the formula with him?"

The butler hesitated for a moment, then nodded.

"I believe that is his custom, sir," he said. "I believe also that that was the main reason for his trip to Brazil."

"O.K. Let's go."

They ran down the marble steps and hurried back to the taxi. "Floyd Bennet field," he ordered.

THROUGH THE streets of New York and over into Brooklyn the cab sped. At the field, they ran into the office of the field manager. There was a night man in charge.

"We want to charter the fastest plane on the field. It's got to be a water job."

The night man shook his head.

"I'm sorry," he said, "but the only water job we've got with any speed was chartered about three hours ago. It was a twin motor Duck."

"You mean one of these Sikorsky amphibians?" Kildare asked.

"That's right, sir," the man replied.

"Where can we get a faster job?"

"There's a Northrup pontoon job up at College Point," he said finally. "I know the guy who owns it. Shall I call and see if he will take you?"

The phone call was made and when he had hung up the night man nodded.

"He'll get over to College Point as soon as he can," he explained.

"O.K., thanks," Kildare said.

They climbed back in the taxi and were whirled over to College Point where Kildare fumed and paced the floor of the office while they waited for the pilot.

"Kildare," Hazard ventured, "I haven't been able yet to figure out how Wu Fang works with those beasts. What do you suppose it was he had on that stick? They seemed to be afraid of it."

"Oh, that. It's simple to me. Apparently, the cloth tied to one end of it, was soaked in some fluid that is distasteful to the little beasts. In all probability, that's how Fu Fang keeps from being attacked by them. He and his agents probably cover themselves with a liquid that the animals don't like."

Hazard nodded.

"I guess that explains it pretty well."

Just then they heard the rumble of a car outside and a sleepy-eyed young man came in, blinking in the light of the office.

"Are you the party that wants to charter the Northrup?" he asked.

Kildare nodded.

"Yes, and there's no time to lose. Get your ship warmed and we'll take off at once."

The pilot hesitated until Kildare flashed his badge of authority.

"O.K.," he said. "I'll be ready in ten minutes."

The pilot was as good as his promise. In ten minutes, they were thundering out across the bay, lifting into the air.

The storm had let up and the stars were peeping through the drifts of clouds.

"I think the weather is going to break," the pilot ventured.

"Let's hope so," Kildare agreed. "We are looking for a yacht named The Nordic. She's a fast craft and is headed south for Brazil. She left New York about thirty-six hours, which would mean that she's down off the Carolinas somewhere. How's your gas supply?"

"If everything works right," the pilot answered, "I can make a good fifteen hundred miles without stopping."

"What's your speed?"

"A little better than two hundred and ten wide open."

Cappy's eyes widened. "Gee, two hundred and ten miles an hour," he breathed.

"That's fine," Kildare commended. "Keep her wide open."

"We won't be able to make fifteen hundred miles wide open on what gas we've got," the pilot objected, "and the motor is more apt to hold together in good shape if we cruise at a hundred and eighty or ninety."

"The speed is what we're after," Kildare said. "Leave her wide open until after daylight, anyway."

Then, as they thundered on toward the darkness he turned to face the others.

"It strikes me," he said, "that this is a good time to catch up on some sleep. We won't be able to do a thing until we get down past the Carolinas. By the way, have you got a wireless set on board?"

The pilot nodded. "Two-way voice hook-up."

"O.K., well probably use that in the morning when we get farther down the coast," Kildare said.

HAZARD LOLLED back in the seat and tried to sleep. For a time, he thought slumber would never come but gradually it overtook him and his weary brain lapsed into oblivion.

When he awoke, it was broad daylight. The sun had been up perhaps two hours or more. The sky was clear and the great yellow disc was blazing down at them from far across the ocean to the east.

On their right, they could see the thin shore line. Kildare was already awake. He unwrapped a package of sandwiches that he had secured at the field, and passed them around.

"We may not get a chance to eat much on this trip, so we'll do it now," he said.

Then for the first time, Hazard realized that he was actually hungry. Up there in the clear morning air, all the horrors of the night before seemed to diminish. When they had finished their scanty repast, Kildare leaned over to the pilot.

"See if you can contact The Nordic," he ordered. "If you get them, let me talk."

The pilot threw a switch, made adjustments on his radio set, clamped the earphones on his head and turned to the mouthpiece before him.

"Plane NC2961-R calling yacht Nordic," he said. "Plane NC2961-R calling yacht Nordic."

Again and again the pilot repeated that call.

"I've got both sending and receiving sets," he explained. "If The Nordic is like most other ships, it has only a buzzer wireless. That is, one that sends messages in code. I've got to run over the dials to see if they answer."

For a long time, they continued to fly on down the coast. Now and then at frequent intervals, the pilot repeated his call. It was getting toward noon when he straightened suddenly. "I've got something!" he said. He listened intently, then gave a short nod.

"Yep," he exclaimed. "I've got the Nordic. That's just luck. Someone on the yacht must have been fooling around with the short-wave radio, trying to pick up some outside stuff and happened to horn in on us. The Nordic says to go ahead."

He handed the mouthpiece to Kildare.

"Hello, Nordic. Have Mr. Darien come to the radio at once."
He repeated that again and again until the pilot nodded.

"They just answered in code," the pilot said. "They say Darien's
at the radio."

"Inspector Kildare of the Federal Bureau," Kildare went on.
"Be very careful. Warn your crew. A twin-motor Sikorsky
amphibian, carrying Wu Fang and agents, is following you.
They want the Opporte invention formula. Don't allow them
on board. We're coming as fast as we can. Do you understand?"

He watched the pilot as he listened for the return code
message. Minutes passed. A perplexed look came over the pilot's
face. At length, he turned to Kildare.

"That's funny," he said. "They don't answer. At least, they
ought to say O.K. and sign off."

CHAPTER 19
DEAD MAN'S YACHT

FRANTICALLY, KILDARE clutched the mouthpiece
and repeated the message twice; each time, he asked, "Do
you understand? Answer by wireless at once." But there was no
reply.

"Something's happened," Kildare groaned. "Give that engine
of yours all she's got, pilot. We've got to get there in a hurry.
Have you any idea where The Nordic is?"

The pilot shook his head. "No, but she can't be a great distance
away now. Down along the north Florida coast, perhaps. We're
about opposite Savannah now."

They droned on and presently he pointed to the gas gauge.

"We haven't more than an hour's gas left," he said, "possibly an hour and a half. We'll have to stop somewhere before long and fill up."

"Keep going," Kildare said savagely.

It was perhaps five minutes after Kildare said that that the pilot jerked upright in his seat and stared through the windshield. He pointed down.

"There's a yacht down there, but it doesn't seem to be moving."

As he spoke, he dropped the plane's nose and aimed it straight for the floating, elongated speck on the water. All eyes were strained upon that craft as they neared it.

"It isn't moving," Kildare admitted. "It's drifting—Good Lord! It looks like there's a hole in the top of those upper cabins. Yes, that's The Nordic all right. We're too late."

"Looks like somebody dropped a bomb on her or something," the pilot ventured.

They were close enough now to see the yacht in detail. There was no sign of life on deck, although several human beings were visible, stretched out on the surface of it. Fear gripping his heart, Kildare sat silently until the amphibian landed. Rocking gently in the low swells of the sea, it pulled alongside the boat.

"Not a living soul in sight," Hazard cracked. "That devil has been here before us."

The three swiftly clambered aboard the palatial yacht while the pilot made his plane fast. As they raced over the deck, Kildare glanced at members of the Nordic's crew.

"It's Wu Fang all right," he groaned. "He turned his beasts loose on the crew while he argued about coming aboard."

He dived down a stairway and then stopped short as he came to the door of a cabin in the center. The door had been smashed down, although the thick panels of plate glass in it were still intact.

A man with gray hair sat slumped over a desk. Kildare turned quickly to Hazard.

"Do you know Darien by sight?"

Hazard nodded. Walking over to the dead man he rolled the head so that he could see his face.

"Yes," he said, "this is Darien."

Kildare bit his lip. He stood there, studying the desk and the room.

"H'm," he said half aloud, "that's interesting. There's a double penholder and one of the pens is lying on the desk; also there's a burned match and—"

He stopped. Leaning over, be pulled the fingers of Darien's right hand open. It had apparently been clutching something for the palm was black.

"Good Lord!" breathed Hazard. "Is that another of Wu Fang's horrors?"

Kildare shook his head.

"It's something else, I believe. Look, this is charred paper. It looks as though Darien had burned a piece of paper and then crushed it in the palm of his hand Also, do you see that pen lying on the desk? That isn't in its proper place. It should be in the holder with the handle sticking upright at an angle. It's my guess that Darien was writing something just before he died."

He searched the desk top. Then suddenly, his eyes fell upon a small book. On the cover of it was printed in great letters, "Ship's Log." He opened it hurriedly to the last page that contained writing and stared. There in an easy-flowing band, words were set down, apparently written in great haste.

Federal Agent Kildare:

A few minutes before writing this I received your warning. Before I could signal an O.K. I heard a plane overhead. Then there was an explosion—I think we were bombed. The bomb was cleverly placed so that it stalled our engines. I rushed out on deck—and there, swarming all over, were the most ghastly creatures I have ever seen. Snakes, lizards, and other horrible things. Even now as I write, I can bear the cries of pain as the members of my crew die in torment. But I realize that I have even a greater duty to carry out. I have here with me a gallon bottle of the liquid gas which George Opporte invented. I have also here the formula for this liquid. I have locked myself in. I am becoming drowsy. I believe I am being drugged with gas. I will stop now and burn the formula so that the horrible secret of this deadly gas will be gone forever.

Marcus Darien.

KILDARE PICKED the log book up and tucked it under his arm.

"Well," Hazard said, "that seems to be the end of it. The secret formula was destroyed."

"End?" Kildare demanded. His lips settled into harsh lines before he went on quietly.

"We've got the biggest job of all to do yet. Wu Fang is loose with a whole gallon of that liquid. I may be crazy, but I guess he is heading back to New York. He is going to try to kill the entire population of New York with that murderous gas. If he succeeds, then he can make his own terms with the rest of the world. If he kills the whole population of New York, he will, in all probability, kill us too for we'll be there trying to stop him."

Before he finished speaking, he was already pacing out on deck again. He leaped to the pontoon of the low-winged monoplane.

"Quick!" he shouted, "we've got to get back to New York."

The pilot shook his head. "We've got to stop for gas first. I think we can make Savannah."

Kildare nodded and the three piled in. As the plane soared into the air, Hazard ventured—

"That's just a guess of yours that Wu Fang is headed for New York, isn't it?"

Kildare frowned. "Yes. But I'm going to check up along the coast when we stop at Savannah."

He did. While the plane was taking on fuel, he phoned Charleston and after a few minutes of conversation, turned with satisfaction.

"We're on the right track," he said. "That Sikorsky amphibian stopped at Charleston to gas up on the way down and it just returned a little while ago. It was headed north up the coast.

Wu Fang is going to New York and pilot, it's your job to catch him before he gets there."

"I'll do my best," the pilot said.

A few moments later they were thundering through the afternoon skies again. As dusk came the pilot pointed far ahead up the south Jersey coast, to a speck in the dim skies.

"That's the Sikorsky," he nodded.

"Can you catch her before she reaches New York?" Kildare asked.

The pilot shrugged.

"I don't know," he said. "We're about a hundred and fifty miles from New York and we won't be there for three-quarters of an hour. It will be dark long before then."

Kildare growled, "That won't do. We can't lose the ship in the dark. We can't let them know we're following them, either. Do you suppose they've seen us?"

"They can't look back from one of those jobs without turning," the pilot answered. "And if they're trying to make time, they're not likely to do that."

Kildare slumped back in his seat. His face was expressionless, his eyes stared out vacantly across the ocean.

In the distance now the glow of New York lights became visible. The pilot pointed.

"The Sikorsky's turned on her light!" he exclaimed. "That will make it easy for us to follow her."

"Right," snapped Kildare. "Leave ours off."

Fifteen minutes later, the pilot said—"She's going to try to land in the river."

"Then land beside her. If possible, land between her and the shore." Suddenly, Kildare sat sharply in his seat, uttered a curse deep down in his throat. "I've tried to figure out how Wu Fang would spread that stuff through New York," he said, "ever since we left Savannah. Now I have it!"

He whirled to Hazard.

"Do you know how the buildings in New York are heated?" he demanded.

Hazard's face whitened as a sudden realization of what Kildare was going to say flooded over him.

"You—you mean the main steam generating plant at the edge of the river?"

Kildare gave a short, vicious nod.

"Yes. If Wu Fang can pour that gallon of liquid into the boilers, it will be spread in the steam into every radiator in New York. People will die by the millions. And that's exactly what he's headed for—the great steam plant alongside the river. Remember," he snapped to the pilot. "Land between that plane and the generating plant."

"I'll do the best I can," the pilot promised. "It's pretty dark to make a decent landing."

They waited tensely—Kildare, Hazard, and Cappy—bolt upright in their seats. As the big Northrup monoplane slid down with idling motor they made out the dim form of the Sikorsky just touching the water.

Then suddenly, there was an explosion!

"They've crashed!" Kildare yelled. "That Sikorsky has crashed!"

At that moment, there was a pounding sound as the pontoons

of the Northrup struck the crest of a wave in the river and bounced a little. The pilot was struggling to hold her off; then she settled down with a *plunk* and slowed quickly.

Kildare was already at the door. He threw it open, leaped out on a floating pontoon. It was pitch black; the dim, blinking lights on either side of the shore only seemed to blind him. He could distinguish a great wing projecting above the surface of the river and then, from the crashed Sikorsky, a cry split the night.

"Help! Help!"

The sound of that voice grasped Hazard as though in icy fingers. He had heard it only a few times before but he was sure of its owner.

CHAPTER 20
DEATH OVER MANHATTAN

WITHOUT AN instant's hesitation and before Kildare could stop him, Hazard shed his coat and plunged into the black, swirling water. The cry came again.

"Help!" He struck out like mad for the spot. All about him sounds were rising now in a deafening din. There were the toots of tug boats puffing to the rescue, the sirens of police boats racing up stream.

"Help! Help!"

A hundred feet away now! Hazard was striking the water in a strong overhand stroke with all his might. For the moment, everything else was forgotten except that cry for help in the familiar voice of the beautiful girl that he couldn't forget.

"Hang on!" he called out. "Keep up, Mohra! I'm coming for you."

Then he reached her, had one arm around her and was turning toward shore. He felt something crawling up on him, up his back toward his neck. He heard Mohra cry out. Then she whirled suddenly, struck at the thing and it vanished in the darkness.

"I—I can swim a very little," she gasped.

The water was full of swimmers, deadly little creatures that tried to crawl up on them for support and safety. Murderous things that had to be knocked off with bare hands. Things that crept and clawed for aid with the desperate panic of the drowning.

The docks were suddenly lined with people. Hands helped them ashore and Mohra clung to Hazard frantically.

"Quick!" she breathed. "I must get you away from here, out of the crowd."

Then—Hazard didn't know just why—he was obeying the girl and running with her up a dock. Near the steam plant she stopped, turned to him. Her voice was vibrant with fear.

"You—you saved my life. You are very brave. I—I can't thank you enough or tell you how much I appreciate—"

Then the throng of curiosity seekers was upon them.

Mohra was pushing away from him. When the throng swept she had vanished.

Then a booming cry rang out from the entrance to the power house not fifty feet away. It was Kildare's voice.

"Hazard! Hazard!" he was yelling.

"Coming," Hazard shouted.

He reached the great entrance just as Kildare was slamming shut the iron door in the front section.

"It's been done," Kildare explained hastily. "Wu Fang is in there. A whole bunch of them swam ashore from that Sikorsky. I saw one of Wu Fang's agents holding the bottle, but I couldn't get him quickly enough. They killed the guards at the door, poured the stuff into the boiler of this section and jammed the safety valve so that it will have to go through the steam pipes. But we've got them locked in. There's just one more job, Hazard, before we finish this thing. This man here"—he turned to a man standing beside him in the darkness—"is one of the workmen. He knows where the shut-off valves are that turn off and on the steam mains leading from this section into the city. If we succeed in turning them off—Come on."

They dashed out, raced up a side street that brought them to the back of the building. Led by the workman, they pushed through a small door, down some steps and found themselves in the midst of massive machinery. The great wheels that operated the valves inside the steam pipes were here.

Hazard stopped for a moment and stared as he finished turning the valve that had been allotted to him—stared up at the heavy windows above reinforced with strong wires.

A ghastly half-naked, flat-headed man was on the other side of one of those windows. He was hammering at it—but hammering in vain. He couldn't break the strong wires that were in the glass.

THE CASE OF THE SIX COFFINS

"They're done!" Kildare said. "We've one more job now. We've got to save all the people we can. Follow me."

They raced back to the front of the generating plant and out on the docks. Kildare raised his voice in a sharp command and Cappy and Hazard did the same.

"Get back! Run for your lives! Get off the river front. Pilot, get your plane out of the way before it's too late. A section of the steam plant is going to blow up any minute."

Then, as the throng suddenly turned, Kildare, Hazard and Cappy were caught up and raced along with it. Minutes later, when the waterfront had been cleared and everyone was several blocks away, the ground under their feet shook; there was a great rumbling sound, then a blast as the huge boiler exploded.

"I think," Kildare ventured, "that's finished. And let's hope that Wu Fang was in there when she blew up."

"But the gas!" protested Hazard.

Kildare nodded.

"Yes," he said. "I'm only hoping that after it is mixed with water and flows into the river—as it undoubtedly will—it won't volatize into the deadly gas."

His guess turned out to be true. There were no fatalities from the gas.

Kildare rode with Hazard and Cappy as far as Hazard's newspaper syndicate office and then left them for his quarters.

"Gee," Cappy said as Hazard and he reached the sidewalk, "you have sure got a story to write now."

"I'll say," grinned Hazard, "and I'll lay you a bet, kid, that you'll sell more newspapers tomorrow morning than you ever sold before in your life."

Hazard worked on his story until well past midnight. Finally, when his fingers were sore from constant pounding on typewriter keys and his eyes were red from loss of sleep, his chief rushed in.

"Say, look here, Hazard," he said. "There was that girl angle we got from the police when they raided that joint in Chinatown—remember?"

Hazard nodded dully.

"Play it up good and strong. White girl, mistress of Wu Fang, aids fiend in his work."

Jerry Hazard jumped and shot a savage glance at his chief. Then he got hold of himself and nodded.

"I think you're wrong there, chief," he said quickly. "You haven't read all my story yet. You see, that girl helped us escape when we were tied up in the hold of The Bergenland. She was only being punished there in Chinatown by Wu Fang. I am sure she has no direct connection with Wu Fang, at least not of her own free will—*I hope.*"

Those last two words were not uttered aloud.